I0637912

The Dark Phoenix

The Dark Phoenix

By

Clay F. Turner

Edited

By

Jeanne Mason

Cover Design

By

Sophie Hedge

Turner House Publishing
606 South Main Street
Leachville, AR 72438

First printing, 2017

ISBN 978-0-6925-4685-7

Contents

To the kids who embrace power and for those still trying to find it.

Prologue

Zander

I'm whole again. But where am I? In the middle of—a coffin? Aw, man, they put me in a coffin. Cool! This is going to be fun to bust out of.

Let's see. No room to move, so I'll just spread my energy throughout my body. The heat is accumulating in my hands. Ahh, it's good to feel power again.

Close your eyes and focus, Zander. Release a small amount of fire—just enough to destroy this coffin—but don't let anyone detect you, and don't destroy anyone else's coffin. That's all I need. Okay—*Boosh!*

Pine slats are collapsing around me. Please let the coffins on both sides be intact. Great! My mini-explosion worked! Now to get above ground . . .

A cemetery. Creepy, especially in this overhead moonlight. So it's the middle of the night. At least no one saw me coming out of the ground like one of those undead things in the horror movies we used to—Loddy! I have to find her!

But how? Loddy is far from Earth. She must be in Kallisto's hands by now.

Hands—my appenda-port! It isn't on my finger. Oh, yeah, I broke that a long time ago. Without my appenda-port, finding Loddy won't be easy, but where can I get another one now? Good question, Zander . . .

1

DISAPPEARANCE

Loddy

"Is she the one?"

"That's the infamous Loddy."

"She looks so normal. What happened?"

"Normal? She nearly killed half the school. Without warning she erupted like a volcano . . ."

Neither Professor Omega nor Calix was in the logic classroom, but everyone else was. They stared at me—again. Being feared was getting old, but I knew that after what they had witnessed the day before, they had a right to be afraid. I was dangerous.

From what Kesta told me, Kallisto had explained that my exploding like that was rare. She blamed my outburst on a blip in my entranx pattern and guaranteed that it would never happen again. Despite the outcry, Kallisto insisted that I would not be accompanied by security personnel, but that I would be monitored while on campus. She stationed a canceller in all my classrooms in addition to positioning them randomly about campus.

One person who could not overcome his curiosity about me was Professor Zazz. Although we had finished our appenda-ports in Aspasian Technology, I was the only one who still could not use hers. Since I had awakened all ten conversion stones during the appenda-port-making process, Professor Zazz wanted to study my project for his personal research. It was not as if I had a choice; I could never have told him he couldn't study my project. Professor Zazz scared me. So until he was done, I was without my appenda-port.

I was sitting there daydreaming when Professor Omega walked in. That he looked like a seven-year-old was still hard to grasp because he was my instructor. He stared at me with those violet eyes. I could tell he used every ounce of his will to turn away. Calix strode in behind him and sat next to me. His pompadour took me by surprise, but it was fitting for his outgoing personality.

"Hey, Loddy."

I smiled. "Hey."

"You feeling better?"

I nodded.

"Everyone," Professor Omega began, "we—" His gaze caught mine. "We are going to—to discuss . . . um . . ." He shook his head and looked away. Staring at the ceiling, he continued. "We are going to discuss the advantages and disadvantages of having a weak mind in battle."

"Talk to you during consummation," Calix whispered. He turned his full attention to Professor Omega.

I noticed that throughout the class, Professor Omega seemed bothered by something. He never looked my way again, which made me certain that whatever was disturbing him had to do with me. After the attack he probably assumed that I was a monster, and he could not stand to be in the same room with me.

But I needed to talk with him about my latest realization concerning Kallisto and Kesta, and about whether or not my aunt and uncle could still be alive—and I also needed to know how I was connected to the Clevists.

When class ended, I waited until it was just Professor Omega and me—and the canceller. I sensed that Professor Omega knew I was there, but he still would not look at me. He gathered his materials in his child-sized bag, then froze in front of his desk, his eyes focused on the floor.

"Is there—is there something you need, Loddy?"

"Yes. I need to discuss an assignment." That was the simplest excuse I could think of with the canceller watching me intently.

"I see." Professor Omega approached me and peered into my eyes.

I stared back, thinking how uncanny it was that he looked so young but was still able to project such a mature expression of fear.

He continued to gaze as if he were memorizing every detail of my face. "Well, unfortunately I cannot explain now. I have somewhere to be, but—I will be more than happy to speak with you at this time tomorrow."

"That will work."

"Wonderful." As he spoke, I thought I saw a twinkle in his eye. "Well, I do hope you have a wonderful rest of your day, Miss Clementine. Until tomorrow."

But he never showed up.

That exchange occurred a week ago, and I still have not seen Professor Omega. I do not believe he is sick or on vacation because he did not tell the class that he would be away. He seemed like the type of person who would warn us before being gone indefinitely.

Surely the canceller had not prompted Kallisto to take action against the professor. After all, Kallisto could not have known about the confidential subjects we had discussed, so she had no reason to surveil him.

But part of my mind thought that that was exactly what had happened. Was Kallisto hiding something and keeping the professor away from me so that I wouldn't find out?

Since my outburst, the Aspasian press had descended on campus trying to interview me or anyone associated with me. Reporters tried to talk with Calix twice, but he refused to tell them anything. The same was true for Carrigan—except that he probably kept his silence more from annoyance than loyalty to me.

The Aspasian Investigatory Force had also started snooping around, but Kallisto was able to stop them before they got to me or my friends. Apparently the AIF was the equivalent of the FBI back in the States, so thwarting them was a coup in itself. Still, it was hard to believe that Kallisto had succeeding in convincing people above her in authority like the AIF to leave without much spectacle.

I was sitting in logic class with the substitute teacher, if one could call him that. Borjaf was a short man with stringy red hair and a large mustache who spoke in a monotone the entire class period. If that was not annoying enough, Borjaf did not teach the material. Instead he rambled on about meaningless blather while most of the class snoozed. I had to listen, though, because I sat in the front row. Not that I would ever snooze during a lecture anyway . . .

But today was different. Before Borjaf got the opportunity to commence with his daily drivel, Kallisto marched in with her trademark air of calm. She wore a sleek black pantsuit, and not a single auburn hair was out of place. Without acknowledging Borjaf, she addressed the class. "I regret to inform you that Professor Omega is on extended leave indefinitely."

What? The mood of the class dropped, but no one dared voice dismay with Kallisto in the room.

Calix leaned over. “I can’t believe this,” he whispered.

“I can’t either. It doesn’t make sense.”

"Professor Omega has not felt like himself for a while,” Kallisto continued. “I suggested that he take a vacation to recuperate. Until then, Borjaf will be your instructor. Thank you.” As soon as she left the room, everyone started talking at once.

I walked to my next class with a sinking feeling that something was horribly wrong. Since I last checked, Kallisto and Kesta had lied about Zander saying he twice tried to murder me, and about Taurik saying he was bad for my reputation.

Besides Taurik, my only other acquaintance who

knew more was Professor Omega. I wanted to find out exactly what he knew before asking Taurik since Kallisto and Kesta were already watching my interactions with Taurik.

Until now, Kallisto had not been monitoring my communication with Professor Omega because she'd had no reason to. But if there was something sinister in the professor's sudden absence—and it felt like there was—Kallisto was probably monitoring us after all. If so, removing the Professor was her way of keeping us from talking.

Another catch was that Taurik thought I was mad at him, so he was avoiding me. What Taurik didn't understand was that I was only pretending to be mad at him to put Kallisto's cancellers, her spies, off my trail.

Without Taurik, I had no way to find the professor. He knew the headmistress better than anyone, and he would know where to start. So until Taurik and I reconnected, I could do nothing. I just hoped that wherever the professor was, he was being treated well.

After sitting through History of Aspasia and Aspasian Technology, I hurried to consummation and sat with Calix and Carrigan. Carrigan was sporting his signature green in the form of a t-shirt. Considering that he was a plant manipulator, it made sense that he always wore green. Calix was still fuming about Professor Omega's indefinite leave.

"I can't believe Omega's away. How are we supposed to learn the essentials of logic now? It's a legitimate fact that Borjaf knows absolutely nothing." Calix rolled his charcoal eyes. Calix' primary concern was always the quality of his schooling. He probably had never considered that Professor Omega might be homebound, sick with some deathly illness.

Carrigan shrugged. "Why do you care? I'd be celebrating if one of my instructors was on extended leave."

"This is our education we're talking about, Carrigan! Don't you want to get the most out of every class here?"

Carrigan stared as if he was surprised to even be having this conversation. "Why am I friends with you?" he asked before returning to what looked like a laffy-taffy fiaszo on his plate.

Calix ignored him as if they were accustomed to having this type of exchange.

"What do *you* think, Loddy? Do you think Professor Omega will ever come back?"

Hmm . . . What do I think about Professor Omega? I fear Kallisto may have scared him away, but he doesn't seem like the kind of person who would back down unless forced to. "I think he'll be back."

At my words, hope gleamed in Calix's eyes. "Really? What makes you say that?"

I was about to explain my reasoning when a blonde glided into the room, looked around, then settled her eyes on mine. She was not Valisa O'Vain, whose parents had taken her out of Abervania the day after the dark phoenix attacked her. To be honest, I couldn't blame them.

No, this blonde was Evily, the one who had been a mystery to me since the first time I saw her. Evily always seemed to be studying me. She was supposed to follow me around and counter the dark energy inside me, but for some reason, she was evading the job. And I thought no one countered Kallisto.

Kallisto hadn't said anything to me about Evily. Of course, I had not seen the headmistress since the attack. It was Kesta who informed me that my training with the headmistress would start the next week, when I would be sure to ask her about Evily.

Evily's avoiding the job made me think she hated me. But something told me that I might not understand her.

Evily's stare did not linger. Her expression changed to one of alarm as if she had just remembered something important, and she rushed out of the room without looking back.

"Loddy!"

I could tell by Calix's tone that this was not the first time he had called my name. I looked over expecting my eyes to settle on him since he was the one addressing me, but instead they settled on Carrigan. He looked frustrated. I dismissed it, figuring his fiaszo may have had a bad taste.

"I'm sorry. I was just—"

"—trying to figure out Evily?" Carrigan sounded bored as his spring-green eyes rested on an unknown subject across the room.

I looked at him with what I hoped was a remorseful expression. "Yes. She bothers me. I wish I knew why she seems so guarded around me."

"It couldn't be because you almost killed a student *and* the headmistress right in front of the student body."

Learning that sarcasm was Carrigan's specialty hadn't taken long. "Thank you. You always know how to make me feel better."

"No problem."

"Look, I know that everyone has every reason to feel guarded around me now, but Evily was like that before, you know?"

Calix nodded.

"I understand," Carrigan said. "But Loddy, you have to remember that Evily acts that way with everyone, not just you."

"I can't help feeling there's more to it." While Calix looked at me with keen interest, Carrigan looked at me with as much interest as he was capable.

An idea popped into my head that I could not believe I had not considered. The answer had been in front of me the whole time—in fact, the answer was *sitting* in front of me right now.

"Calix, would you talk to her for me?"

"What?" Calix's voice dropped an octave.

"I mean, not actually speak to her face-to-face, but do you think you could speak to her mind?" It felt odd asking a question that hinged wholly on my faith in a person's superhuman power, and Calix stared as if that was the last thing he expected me to ask.

"Well, I suppose I could . . ."

Although I sensed that Calix was about to say more, I cut him off. "Great! Let's decide on a place and a time. I wonder, should I be present? I could—"

It was Calix's turn to interrupt. "Loddy, I would love to help you out, and under normal circumstances I could."

"But?" I waited for the negative to issue forth.

"But with the cancellers countering any unsupervised power-use, I can't."

The cancellers. Why hadn't I taken the cancellers into consideration? They were, after all, omnipresent on campus—or so it seemed. "Ah, yes, the cancellers. How could I have forgotten about them? I'll just have to think of something else."

Calix frowned, but he was right. There was nothing in his power that he could do. "I'm sorry, Loddy. We'll try to think of something else, too."

I stood. "I have chastology now. See you later, guys." As I left, I heard Carrigan say, "*He'll* try to."

When I arrived in the chastology classroom, Professor Wakepetal approached me beaming. But in all honesty, his expression was usually enthusiastic.

"Loddy Clementine! How are you today?" His tone was always infused with more happiness than the occasion called for, but it was contagious nonetheless.

I lied. "I am well, Professor."

"I want to ask you something." His plump belly trembled from excitement.

"What is it?"

"Oh, I shouldn't mention it. It isn't any of my business, anyway." For the first time since I'd known him, Professor Wakepetal avoided eye contact. *Is he embarrassed?*

"No, no, Professor. It's fine. What is it?"

"Well, I have noticed during every class that you and Miss Crest go out of each other's way not to speak with each another, and, well, that saddens me."

"Oh, well, sir—"

"I was just wondering—and you don't have to tell me if you don't want to—but why is that?"

"I have no idea, Professor. I wish I did."

"Well, I think both of you would be wonderful together, seeing as you both have such promise, but I guess things take their own time to work themselves out."

"Yes, of course, sir." Other students, including Evily, appeared then and sat on their cloud seats in this classroom in the sky.

"I am sorry to have bothered you, Miss Clementine. You may have a seat." Professor Wakepetal smiled his contagious smile as I took my seat, which happened to be on the opposite side from Evily's. She made sure to put as much distance as possible between us. For the rest of the class, Professor Wakepetal discussed one of the chaste's most powerful abilities: healing.

"Not all chastes can heal," the Professor was saying, "but for those who can, healing proves to be a highly beneficial power, not only for them but for those around them. While healing can instantly change any battle, it is also beneficial outside of battle. Some chastes, like Evily's father, have devoted their lives to healing injured people throughout Aspasia as a sort of doctor. Other chastes may only heal people to a certain degree but are able to save them from death. No chaste can bring a dead person back to life. Many chastes have become aphotics trying to restore life."

I wondered if this was how Taurik had become an aphotic. He seemed too good a person to be one, but this made sense. Unbeknownst to me, during the next few weeks I would learn more about the mysterious Taurik Night than I ever imagined. And this knowledge would accrue in the form of an assignment.

2

100 Questions

Since the attack, Kallisto stationed Canceller Pilmus in the aphotology classroom to prevent the aphotic energy from giving the dark phoenix a foothold in my mind again. Ever since he had been stationed, I hadn't had any more problems controlling myself.

Today I walked into the classroom, which was an actual cave made entirely of stone. Upon entering, one instantly noticed the temperature, which was always cooler than the other classrooms. Since there were no windows, the aphotology classroom was much darker, too. The only light was provided by odd, glowing crystals embedded in the stone. As I made my way to a seat in the back, I scanned the room for Taurik. He was not there yet, but that didn't surprise me. He was always late.

I made a habit of sitting in the back of the aphotology classroom because all the students in the class—except Taurik—scared me. They always scowled at me with sheer hatred or utter disregard. Most dressed in dark colors that only added to their overall creepiness. And since they had witnessed me almost kill another student and the headmistress, I guessed that they weren't any crazier about me now than they had been before. If anything, I was almost sure that they wanted me dead and could easily kill me.

Since sitting in on some of the classes, I realized just how dark aphotics' powers could be. For instance, Taurik's friend with the spiky green hair, Cash, has the ability to cause explosions that paralyze people's entire bodies.

Taurik's other friend, Cassius, has scarlet hair and a permanently depressed expression. His touch infects people's nature to the point that it can make them evil. I was apprehensive whenever I was around him.

The guy with a conspicuous gash on his left arm is Bite. He can suck the light out of any area to make it pure darkness.

Taurik's other friend, a girl called Malicious, has magenta hair. She can whisper secrets into her hand and send them off to her intended listener without having them heard by anyone else. In my opinion, it is every girl's dream to be able to gossip without the fear of being overheard by anyone else. But her power still scared me. It made me wonder what she was whispering about me.

Taurik had one friend, Draegan, whose power remained unknown to me. Draegan has slick, black hair with slight shadings of grey. I didn't think it was possible, but after observing him and Cassius, I realized his depressed expression is even more pronounced than Cassius's.

Even though he never talks, Draegan has an air of intrigue about him. He also wears black gloves all the time, which I don't understand. I suspect that it has to do with his power. I figure his power is at the root of his demeanor, but if the knowledge of possessing such a power causes that much sadness, could it be worse than those of which I'd already heard?

All these powers made me wish I could switch out of the class as soon as possible, but I knew Kallisto wouldn't let me. Aphotology was part of my original curriculum.

Professor Nazzir taught aphotology. He was a small man who supported a hump on his back covered by a black cloak. He always wore an expression of indifference better than anyone. His expression didn't make one feel inferior socially and intellectually, though. Instead, his demeanor made one grow accustomed to seeing his expression as something comforting, which meshed with his personality.

Professor Nazzir was a pleasant man, especially for teaching the most depressing subject ever. He also seemed to genuinely care for his students and expressed a fervent wish that they get as much from his class as they could. At the same time, he always kept his cool and maintained control without seeming domineering.

The professor meandered in soon after I did. Without looking at a single student, he sat at his dilapidated desk whose top had not a single item save for the large, gray book he used to teach our class. This oversized tome was also dilapidated. The odd symbols decorating its cover looked like ancient runes. He flipped the book open and scanned a page before quickly slamming the book shut. He tapped his fingers on the desk and stared at the floor, deliberating with himself. He took a breath, looked up, and addressed us in his usual tenor voice. "Something bothers me about this class." He sounded calm, but it worried me that something bothered him. After all, with him, one never knew what he really meant when he said something like that. His statements were often ambiguous because he never interjected emotion into what he said.

At that moment, Taurik Night decided to make his appearance. Sporting a black T-shirt that accentuated his muscles, he strolled into the classroom without looking at Professor Nazzir, who paused long enough for Taurik to take his seat. As soon as he sat down, Professor Nazzir continued.

I couldn't help but steal a glance at Taurik's messy sable hair and clear salmon eyes.

"I do not think, students, that you realize the opportunity you have before you in a class of this type."

Taurik's eyebrows were knitted together. He hadn't typically frowned when I first met him, but since I'd put on my mad act, he was different. I was ready to tell him the truth.

"Class, I have devised a group project that will enable you to gain rare knowledge from your fellow classmates."

What? A group *project?* I turned my attention from Taurik to Professor Nazzir. A group project meant that I would have to interact with the odd people. Students around the room moaned.

"The project is simply called 100 Questions. You will all be required to answer 100 questions regarding the redeeming as well as the dark qualities exhibited in your partner. The exercise will give us all a new way of seeing each other, and, in turn, a new way of looking at aphotology. *I* will choose the partners, however."

Wonderful.

"How does that sound?"

No one spoke. We just stared at him. I was afraid I was going to be paired with someone who hated me.

"Very well." He began surveying the room with hungry eyes.

I thought I saw a trace of giddiness in them. Could this be the enjoyment he got from his job?

"Cash, I want you with . . . Cassius."

I looked at Cash to see him nodding and smiling at the professor.

"Yes, sir!" Cash said in his lower tenor voice. He then flashed a thumbs up and smiled at Cassius who shrugged.

"Next, I want Malicious with . . . Draegan."

"Oh, really?" Malicious asked. Her voice gushed with happiness. "Thank you, Professor! We'll have a good time, won't we, Draegan?"

Draegan neither said nor did anything to acknowledge that he had heard her.

For the next five minutes, Professor Nazzir assigned everyone else in the classroom partners leaving another girl, Taurik, Bite and me.

"Let me see." Professor Nazzir seemed to be relishing the moment. "Loddy Clementine, with whom do I want to put you?"

I looked up at him and smiled. I didn't want to be

with Bite or the other girl whose name I couldn't remember, but who I knew was among those who gave me death glares every chance she got.

Taurik stood up. "Loddy needs to be with me."

Is this really happening? I could feel myself blush.

The professor turned his attention to Taurik, his expression curious. "Really, Mr. Night? And what makes you say that?" Keen interest sounded in his voice.

Taurik puffed out his chest, perfectly at ease addressing the professor in front of the entire class. "Well, sir, I think you would be denying Bite and Jazda a wonderful opportunity if you put either of them with Loddy or me. You see, Bite is the type of person who doesn't allow anything to get to him. He takes everything as it is, and doesn't worry about changing it in any way. Not that he is smart enough *to* worry."

The entire class—except Cassius and Draegan—guffawed. Even Bite began laughing.

"Now Jazda, on the other hand, is a worrier. She absolutely *must* have control of every situation. That's because she knows that she's intelligent enough to succeed in anything. Right, Jazda?"

Jazda nodded, grinning. As her head bobbed, her stringy teal hair bounced.

"Professor, my point is this: Bite and Jazda are completely different individuals. They do not go about each day with the same objective in mind. Bite's goal is to live life in a way that brings him the most happiness while he disregards any sort of ambitious goals. Jazda's goal is to live life in a way that brings her the most success.

Ambitious goals are her first priority while she disregards her happiness altogether. In turn, both of them suffer because they disregard half of the whole life experience.

"Perhaps, then, if they were able to spend time together, they could learn vital lessons about each other's extreme side to the point that they could begin to integrate aspects of both into their personalities. Then they would be able to abandon their self-destructive behaviors and adopt behaviors that would bring them balance and peace. After all, when polar behaviors coalesce in perfect harmony, people become who God wants them to be, wouldn't you say, Professor?"

The professor nodded thoughtfully.

"Then it should follow that Bite and Jazda should be partners, leaving me with Loddy. I know Loddy wouldn't want to rob Bite and Jazda of this invaluable opportunity to abandon their self-destructive behaviors either—because she knows that would be selfish."

Wow. I had no idea Taurik was a gifted debater. The entire class stared at him while he finished his spiel, and some of them rolled their eyes as if this was regular behavior for him.

Professor Nazzir's eyes became slits as he considered Taurik's argument. "Very well, Mr. Night, Bite and Jazda shall be partners, which means you and Miss Clementine will be paired together. Satisfied?"

"Yes, sir. Thank you, sir."

Pilmus clenched his jaw. My guess was that he didn't want Taurik anywhere near me, and neither did Kallisto. At least I hadn't made a conscious effort to be his partner.

Before leaving aphotology, Taurik made his way over to me. Without making eye contact, he whispered, "I'll meet you outside of the power practice room after today's classes." Then, without waiting for a reply, he left.

So, he was still nervous about talking directly to me. But at least that hadn't stopped him from doing everything imaginable to make me his partner.

I headed to power practice. My team had not won a single match even though Valisa, the opposition's star player, was gone. So now Professor Pex had us partner up and practice hand-to-hand combat every day.

Calix and I always partnered up. While play-fighting, I told him what had happened in aphotology.

"Are you serious?" His voice was more anxious than I expected.

"Yes." I dodged one of his punches. "Taurik clearly wants to partner up with me." I tried to take the moment to kick Calix, but he dodged and grabbed my leg.

"Loddy, Taurik . . . is . . . dangerous. Don't you realize this?"

"I don't know. I find that hard to believe."

Calix grasped my leg with all his might, twisted it, and flung me on to the ground.

"Ow!" Pain rushed through my back. "That hurt!"

"Sorry." He gave me his hand and pulled me up to look him straight in the eye. "Loddy, I just don't want you to get hurt. He seems harmless because that's what he wants you to believe. But when the time comes when you are no longer useful to him, he *will* hurt you. That is what he is designed for."

Designed for? He must be referring to Taurik's supposedly being a morbid. Kallisto had told me that, but I wasn't sure I believed her. "Calix, what are you talking about?"

He looked over at the rest of the class who were still play-fighting before turning his attention back to me. He grabbed my arm and turned me away from the class whispering "Loddy, I don't want to scare you. But Taurik is a morbid, which means he's a deplorable human being."

"Are you sure?" It couldn't be true.

"As sure as I can be."

Great . . . Calix said something else, but I didn't hear him because my attention was centered in on the person who had just walked in. She didn't want to draw attention to herself, but I could tell she had an important reason for being here.

Calix couldn't suppress his curiosity. "Loddy, why is the headmistress here again?"

"I . . . I don't know."

Professor Pex, a large muscular man, spoke to her through big eyes as if he were her student instead of a fellow faculty member. This was the third time she had interrupted a power practice class this week, and I had no idea why.

They spoke briefly before she nodded at him once, glanced at me causing me to freeze, and walked out.

As soon as power practice was over, I told Calix good-bye without mentioning my and Taurik's meeting. I didn't have to wait at all. As soon as Calix left, Taurik appeared looking nervous. He wasted no time getting to the point.

"I heard you were able to transport Kesta into Chaste Palez. Could you transport me inside, too?"

"I think so. Why?"

"I'll meet you there." He looked around. "I'll explain when we're in a less monitored environment."

3

TRUTH

In a matter of minutes, I was outside Chaste Palez's doors contemplating whether I had made the right decision. After all, I could have misinterpreted my thoughts and been wrong about Kallisto and Kesta's lying to me. Maybe I hadn't remembered properly from that dreaded day. Moreover, Calix didn't seem to trust Taurik, either.

"Are you ready?" a voice asked. I looked up to behold Taurik's flawless features, his beautiful smile and those salmon eyes that still held a trace of anxiety. I realized then that I would have trusted him with my life. He would never hurt me. Somehow, Kallisto, Kesta, and Calix all had it wrong.

As soon as we were inside, Taurik's demeanor changed from extreme anxiousness to utter relaxation, and he observed every detail of Chaste Palez.

"Loddy, this place is beautiful. Now I see why chastes have such sunny dispositions."

I laughed. It seemed as if the pretend-fight hadn't even happened now, and Taurik was back to his old self.

"What are you talking about? Don't aphotics have a lobby in their building, too?"

"Sort of."

Then, as if remembering his purpose, he turned off his playful mood. "So, you're talking to me again?"

I tried to make eye contact with him before answering but he turned away. Instead, I said, "Of course, Taurik. I've been meaning to talk to you about that."

"Really?"

He made his way to the floating couches to sit down. I sat next to him. He still wouldn't look at me.

"Yes. You see, I have reason to believe—"

"Taurik Night, what are you doing in Chaste Palez?" Cannon stared in disbelief. Her petite frame was trembling with rage.

"I'm doing an assignment with Loddy for aphotology. Is that okay with you?"

She couldn't stop staring at Taurik. "But how did you get in? No one besides chastes can get into this building. The *headmistress* can't even get into this building."

"I walked in just like the rest of you." Taurik shrugged, as if the answer should have been obvious to her.

Cannon's nostrils flared. She pointed to the exit with a recently-manicured finger. "Taurik Night, *you* get out of our building *now*!"

He raised himself from the couch slightly so that his face was within inches of hers. "No."

Cannon turned to me, her gloss-laden lips pursed. "I'm surprised you're okay with being seen with him after I told you what he did to *me*."

Some of the fight left Taurik's eyes. "Cannon, we're just doing an assignment. That's all." Her expression transitioned to one of sheer hatred as she stared first at Taurik and then at me. This time I felt her rage was targeted more toward me than Taurik.

"Fine, but don't expect this to continue. I doubt the headmistress wants an *aphotic* under the roof of the Chaste Palez." She glared at us, then walked into the glass pod, causing it to illuminate. After the Torggler door shut off her glare, the pod shot upwards until we could no longer make it out.

"Wow," Taurik said, "You chastes even have better transport to your rooms than we do." "I wish she hadn't seen you. You realize we'll have to find another place to meet now?"

He grinned mischievously. "Why do you say that?"

"You know she'll tattle to the headmistress."

"There is another alternative." His playful eyes held me captive.

"Where is that?"

"*Your* room. Of course, you probably don't trust me enough . . ."

"Taurik, I'm not mad at you, and I never was."

He raised his eyebrows.

"The fight . . . It was fake. I had to make Pilmus think I was mad at you so he wouldn't read too much into my being around you. He watches me enough already. If he knew that I trusted you and he told Kallisto and Kesta, they would find a way to prevent me from ever speaking to you again."

"You're serious? So it was all fake?" Taurik's face relaxed.

"Yes."

He sighed and leaned back, shaking his head. "So they *did* try to brainwash you."

"Yes, but I realized one of their stories didn't add up when I ran its timeline through my head." Our eyes met.

"What story was that?"

I told him how Zander's body had been found in a cornfield in Sun City a few months earlier but that I could still hear his voice in my mind, and how Zander's voice had been silenced as soon as I burned down the mansion in which he and I met, how I started a forest fire trying to find him, and how I found the note supposedly from him just before I left Earth. I almost told him about the letter from Meda, but I decided to wait. It wasn't that I didn't trust him; I just felt like I needed to respect her wishes to keep it a secret.

I told him how Kesta and Kallisto made it seem like Zander had tried to kill me through the mansion and the forest fires, but that I realized my enemy had been the dark phoenix all along. The odd part was that the dark phoenix had killed Zander two months before the forest fire, so there was no way Zander could have started the forest or mansion fires.

"Wait a second. *Zander* was your boyfriend?"

Hearing his name hurt. "Yes."

"And this dark phoenix killed him not once but *twice*—using *your* body?"

"Yes." How the events had all played out did sound creepy.

Taurik peered at me intently. "Loddy, did Zander

say anything peculiar while you were around him?"

I paused to reflect on everything Zander had told me. "He did say one thing I still can't make sense of. Before he was silenced, he called me *quizeen*. Kesta said a quizeen is a—"

"—ruler over an entire quasian. Some refer to a quizeen as a princess." He spoke as if he was trying to convince himself that his words were true. He looked at me with reverence, as if seeing me for the first time.

"What is it, Taurik? What's wrong?"

He opened his mouth to speak but decided against it. He opened it again, but shook his head. “I . . . I can’t say.” He sounded disappointed and turned away.

"Why can’t you? She hasn't gotten to you, too, has she?"

He whipped around. "I assure you it's nothing like that. Who else has she gotten to?"

"Professor Omega. A week ago, he and I were supposed to discuss my past, but he hasn't been back since we made our appointment. He said nothing about being gone indefinitely, which is peculiar for him. Why can't you tell me what’s wrong?"

"Did you say that they tried to make it look like Zander killed your aunt and uncle?"

"Yes. Why?"

"There’s a chance they may still be alive.”

“Really?” My heart felt like it could soar out of Aspasia and into deep space. I couldn't contain myself and hugged him. Realizing what I was doing, I backed away. "Sorry."

"It's fine."

"How can I check to see if they're still alive?"

"For starters, you would need an appenda-port."

"Professor Zazz has mine."

"Why? Did you give it to him or did he take it?"

"He took it because he wants to study the one appenda-port in history that has all ten conversion stones in it."

"Oh. How *did* you do that, by the way?"

I shrugged and shook my head. "I don't know."

"Well, until you get that appenda-port, we can't go anywhere."

"Why not? Kesta transported us here with hers, and Professor Wakepetal transported twenty students into his class—wait! You're going with me?"

"They can perform those transports because they're older. The older people get, the more entranx energy their appenda-ports can support. I can't support two people with mine, so we'll have to use both of ours. And of course, I can't let you go to another galaxy all alone." He winked.

"Okay, I'll get my appenda-port. Now can you expand more on the *quizeen* thing?"

His expression changed from playful to serious. "No, Loddy, I can't."

"Why not?"

"Because it's a secret."

"A secret?" I glared at him. "But it pertains to *me*!"

"Loddy, shh!" He looked around to see if anyone had heard me.

I stared at him with the most intensity I could

muster. "No! You don't tell me to shush in my own palez."

He grabbed my shoulders. "Loddy, I'll explain why I can't tell you if you'll settle down." I wanted to shrug his hand off, but they felt comfortable. All I could feel, all I could register was the slight pressure he was applying to my shoulders. "Fine."

He let go of my shoulders and leaned back. "You know that I am a morbid, right?"

I withheld my disbelief. "I have heard."

"Did you also know that morbids are sworn from telling secrets?"

"No." That Kallisto would forget to include such critical information was unthinkable. "Kallisto omitted that detail in our briefing."

"Of course she did." Dark sarcasm filled his tone. "She was probably hoping that you would force me to tell a secret."

"But, Taurik, what would be so bad about that? Kallisto isn't around, and I wouldn't tell her anything you told me."

"Loddy, it isn't that simple."

"Why not? Because—"

His dark grin became grim. His expression scared me so much that all my anger for him dissipated, and I only wished to make that scowl disappear.

"—if a morbid tells a secret, he or she dies."

"You're not serious."

"I am." He spoke with such conviction that I could feel the anguish he had gone through accepting this reality about himself.

We sat for a while before either of us spoke.

"I don't understand. morbids are terrible people, right?"

He turned to me, and I saw the face of a little boy staring back, his eyes as vulnerable as if someone had just scolded him. "Loddy, you have to understand that not every morbid has selfish intentions in becoming one. Some morbids do hunger for power and stop at nothing to control everyone and everything around them. Then there are those morbids who protect those around them. I—"

Jevasa's shrill voice sounded over the intercom. "Taurik Night, please report to the orgratium at the front desk."

Oh no . . .

"Cannon works fast, doesn't she?"

"Warp speed. I hope you aren't in trouble."

"Don't worry. It won't be the first time." I followed him to the front desk.

Jevasa regarded Taurik with disdain. When she saw me, the smugness faltered and nervousness took over. She struggled to appear stern as she addressed Taurik. "Taurik Night, it has come to my attention that you are not an occupant of the Chaste Palez."

"Really?" Taurik's voice had an edge of flirtatiousness. Pure appeal began to swim in his eyes, and Jevasa didn't look away.

"Really, I . . . I must ask you to—"

"You're not going to ask me to leave, are you?" His voice was filled with innocence as he feigned disappointment.

Jevasa was about to start drooling. "Of course not." She didn't know what she was saying. "You may stay as long as you want. Is there anything I can get for you?"

The appeal disappeared from Taurik's eyes. "No. But you can let Cannon know that she's a pain."

Jevasa nodded not knowing where she was.

We returned to the couch, and I gaped at him in disbelief. He was fascinating in a dark, mischievous way.

He smiled. "What?"

"You scare me."

"Is that a good thing or a bad thing?"

"I don't know yet."

"I love your eyes, Loddy."

I blushed.

"They remind me of sparkling red wine set against sunlight. It's like they have their own light source."

My cheeks burned as my blush deepened.

"Don't you think we should start on that one-hundred question assignment now?"

The assignment! If we hadn't answered one question, I would have been fine. "Um, sure—but wait! You still haven't told me about the other type of morbid, the type you are."

"Oh." He sounded disappointed. "Um, why don't I tell you about that some other time?" "No. I want to know now. I'm intrigued." I smiled to encourage him.

He smiled back half-heartedly, but his eyes were playful. "No, I think I want to leave you wanting more."

"Ugh! Taurik, *please*!"

"No, Miss Clementine. We must do our homework

like good little aphotic students."

I sighed. Clearly I wasn't to learn anything else about that particular topic right then. "Fine, but I still want to know."

"As you will, I'm sure." He pulled a silver contraption from his pocket that reminded me of a small iPod. He placed it on the table and pushed the middle button on top. A blue screen shot out to display an image of a folder containing papers. He touched the folder, and it materialized in front of us.

"What is *that*?"

"You've never seen a bilbop?"

"No. Does it just store things?"

"Pretty much. But it can store anything."

"Anything?"

"Yes. Now let's get to those questions, okay?"

"Okay."

After an hour, we had only finished ten questions. Taurik had to get back to Aphotology Palez to meet the Aphotic Theory study group, so I walked him to the palez doors.

"I had a great time tonight, Loddy. Are you going to let me come back?"

"I guess—if you're good." I smiled, and he smiled back.

"Not a chance." He turned to leave but stopped, his eyebrows knit. "Loddy, we *will* find your aunt and uncle if they're out there. In the meantime, I wouldn't worry about Kallisto. She's nothing to be afraid of."

"That's easy for you to say. You can talk to her

however you want, and she still lets you roam her school."

"Yep. So are we doing this again tomorrow? We only finished a few questions."

"Sure. Same time?"

"Same time. I will see you tomorrow, Miss Clementine." He bowed. Then, his back to me, he called, "Be careful who you talk to about this, okay?"

"I will."

As I walked to the glass pod, I wondered if what I was doing was right. I knew Taurik and I were just doing an assignment, but I also sensed that our friendship could develop into something more. In fact, I could see our relationship going somewhere very soon. Why did I feel guilty? Zander was dead, and any chance of my seeing him again had been destroyed the moment the dark phoenix killed him. Maybe my heart hadn't caught up with my head yet—or was I grasping at the one last hope that Zander might still be alive?

Taurik

I rushed into Kallisto's office, not caring whether she had a visitor. "She has a *boyfriend*?"

She didn't look up. "*Had* a boyfriend."

"Why didn't you tell me?"

"The same reason you failed to mention that you and she were lab partners."

Of course. "You already know about that."

Our eyes met. "Mr. Night, do you have a reason for

being here?"

"Yes." My heart beat furiously. "I can't do this anymore. Keep your secrets."

Kallisto sauntered toward me, never breaking eye contact. "You must. This is the path you chose for your little . . . Persi."

"*Her name is Persephone*. You know that."

"Whatever."

"You know Loddy's going to figure out her true identity. If it isn't I who tells her, someone will."

She sniggered. "We've made sure that won't happen."

"By kidnapping one of your own faculty members?"

Her back toward me, she froze. "I'm sure I don't know of what you speak."

"I just hope you're feeding him." I started for the exit.

"Mr. Night?"

I stopped. "What?"

"I hope you haven't forgotten your place. I can make your life very difficult." Malice enlaced her tone.

"Doubt it."

"You can enjoy your time with her now. But be mindful that it won't last. I always get what I want."

I grinned as I placed my appenda-port into the console. As I disappeared, one thought encircled my mind: *So do I.*

4

PHOENIX SPIRITS

Zander

I was trapped. I couldn't make an appenda-port because conversion stones could only be found in Aspasia. So I decided to visit Uncle William and Aunt Maggie to figure out what happened to Loddy. I hoped they still lived in the same place . . .

Loddy

The next morning, I met Calix and Carrigan at the Pinkest Pokest eatery. Since Calix had suggested the idea, we three had been meeting together almost every morning to talk. I enjoyed their company, but for some reason, I hadn't told them my secret fears concerning Kallisto. However, I could see myself opening up to Calix soon. He seemed interested in all I had to say, and besides that, he was a loyal friend. Carrigan seemed indifferent to what I had to say, but I felt he was loyal to me.

Before I reached the Pinkest Pokest, I spotted Cannon sitting alone at Callaway's eatery. *I've never seen Cannon at Callaway's before. And alone. Maybe she's waiting for me.* The second she saw me, she lit up and signaled me to join her. I obliged, though reluctantly. The last time I checked, she was mad at me for letting Taurik into Chaste Palez.

When I reached her table, her effervescence did not fade as I'd thought it would. If anything, she became more animated.

"Hey, Loddy!" she exclaimed.

"Hey, Cannon." I was guarded.

"Sit down!" She signaled to the seat across from her.

"Sure . . ."

"So, how are you?"

"I'm well. And you?"

"Just wonderful."

I had a feeling she was making small-talk before discussing what was really on her mind, so I took control of the conversation. "Did you need something?"

"Well," she said, twirling her hair, "I realize I wasn't as, um, warm to you as I should have been last night."

Ahh. So you're going to butter me up. I decided to play along. I figured it would make the conversation progress faster.

"Oh, that's fine. I can see how a student could get territorial over his or her palez."

"Yes. Well, I guess what I'm trying to say is I'm sorry. I shouldn't have acted that way toward you."

"Cannon, it's fine. Really. I'm not mad at all." I rose from my chair. "Now if you'll excuse me, I have someone—"

She grabbed my arm. "You're not going to leave without telling me what you and Taurik talked about, are you?"

There it is. I looked Cannon in the eye and smiled as warmly as I could. "Yes, I am."

She stood.

I walked away, but she followed.

"Why?" she demanded. "Why won't you tell me? Don't you trust me?"

I turned. "I don't know, Cannon. Hey! Maybe I'm still trying to figure you out." I tried to sound like I was joking, but I was dead serious. Something told me I shouldn't tell her anything about my personal life.

"What do you mean? I told *you* one of the most private confidences in my life *in front of the headmistress*. I was trying to *protect* you, Loddy."

Ugh. I didn't feel like dealing with her so early in the morning. "Cannon, I know, and I appreciate that. But I have to meet someone."

I walked away sure that she was bashing me in her mind.

She called after me. "The least you could do is come see me at the duel on Friday."

I stopped. "What time?"

"Seven."

I decided that accepting her invitation would make things easier. "I'll be there."

"Wonderful! See you then."

When I reached the Pinkest Pokest, Calix and Carrigan were seated in the back of our hang-out spot.

Calix waved me over. Per usual, Mr. Barboo stood in the middle of the eatery wearing his smudged apron and handing out drinks, but as I passed him, he stopped me.

"Miss Clementine, what a pleasure to see you." I knew he was eager for information about Professor Omega. Ever since the professor had gone missing, Mr. Barboo had interrogated me as to his whereabouts almost every day.

"It is a pleasure to see you as well, Mr. Barboo."

"Follow me, please." He led me to a corner of the eatery, where he sat his tray down on the counter, then turned to me with eager eyes. He was an oversized man, so he took up more of the corner than a regular-sized person would have. "So? Anything?"

"No, sir. I'm afraid not."

The eagerness left his baggy eyes. "I see." His sad tone reminded me of one who has lost a loved one. I wished I could have provided him with some information, but I had no leads.

"Mr. Barboo, not that I don't enjoy our chats, but I was wondering: Why do you ask me, of all people, about Professor Omega? Surely you know professors who are more in-the-know than I?"

"Not really, Miss Clementine. Professor Omega was the only professor who talked to me as a friend. All the other professors either eat at other eateries or they pay me no mind while they're here. And besides, *you* are the most talked-about student at Abervania now. I figured if anyone was in the loop, it would be you."

I blushed. "Mr. Barboo, that isn't true. People don't think I'm in the loop. They think I'm weird."

"Oh, no, Miss Clementine. Although the rest of Aspasia is talking about you, too. Surely you've heard?"

"Yes, sir." I looked to see that Calix was patiently waiting for me while Carrigan drummed his fingers on the table.

"Sir, I need to get to my table. My friends have been waiting for me."

"Oh, yes, of course." I could tell he had forgotten his other customers. "Go on. I will talk to you later. Have a wonderful day, Miss Clementine."

I sat down next to Carrigan. Only Calix was smiling.

"Couldn't get away, could you?" Calix joked.

"No. He wanted to know if I knew anything about Professor Omega."

"Well, do you?"

"No. How could I? I know just as much as everyone else."

At that moment, a waiter approached our table. His face was tattooed with the familiar runes that emblazoned all the workers' faces.

"You all go ahead and order. I kept you waiting long enough," I said.

Carrigan opened his mouth to order, but Calix interjected, "It is perfectly fine, Loddy. We can wait a bit longer. No big deal." He looked at the waiter. "Could you give us a few more minutes?" The waiter nodded before walking off. I could hear Carrigan fuming beside me.

"Oh, sure, we can wait. It isn't like we haven't already waited long enough to memorize the entire menu."

"Stop, Carrigan," Calix said. "Loddy was just running late, right?"

"Well, actually—"

Carrigan interrupted with forced civility. "Figure out what you want to order and then talk. *Please.*"

"Okay, no problem." I looked over the menu and decided on a Pinkest Pucker. Ever since Cannon had introduced me to this marvelous drink, I'd had to have one every time I came to the Pinkest Pokest. "I know what I want."

"Thank goodness," Carrigan said.

"Don't mind him," Calix said. "Did you oversleep?"

"No. Cannon stopped me, and I couldn't get away from her."

Carrigan's eyes shifted from the dessert listings to me. I don't know why I hadn't noticed before, but it looked like perspiration running down his brow. "Carrigan, what's wrong?" I asked.

His eyes dilated as if he had been caught in the middle of a lie. "Why?"

"Sweat is running down your face."

He looked puzzled as he brought his hand up to his brow. His expression remained baffled as his hand brushed away the sweat. "Hmm, that is odd. Where is that waiter? I'm ready to order."

As if on cue, the waiter reappeared and took our order.

When he left, Calix asked, "What did Cannon want?"

"She wanted to know what Taurik and I talked

about last night during our questionnaire session."

"Questionnaire session *last night*? You went through with it?"

"Well, yes, Calix. It isn't like I can dodge an assignment just because you don't like my partner."

"Get a new partner! Can't you do that?"

"How? Tell Professor Nazzir I don't agree with his pairings?"

"So what *did* you guys talk about?"

Carrigan's question surprised me. I didn't think he was interested in the minute details of my life. Beyond that, I wasn't sure if I wanted to tell him and Calix the secret happenings in my life because I wasn't sure how they would handle them. Before I could think further, I realized I was talking. "Do you guys remember how Kallisto told everyone that the reason behind my explosion was a blip in my entranx pattern?"

They nodded, their foreheads creasing.

"That was just a cover."

"Are you saying our headmistress lied to everyone?" Calix asked.

"More or less . . ."

"Oh, wow," Calix said.

Carrigan's expression didn't change. "So what caused your explosion?"

The waiter delivered our food and drinks. After making sure that we didn't need anything else, he left.

"Do both of you know what a dark phoenix is?" Disbelief registered in their eyes as they realized what I was about to tell them.

"You're not saying—" Carrigan began.

"Yes. It's true. I have a dark phoenix inside me."

"Wait. Is that what you were talking about when we were in the hospital wing?" Calix asked.

"What do you mean?"

"You told me that you never know what's going to happen when you black out. Did you mean you never know what the dark phoenix is going to do?"

I had forgotten about that. "Oh, yes. That was what I was talking about." I sipped my Pinkest Pucker and savored the wonderful tang of liquidized strawberry.

"What does Taurik Night have to do with it?" I detected a hint of sarcasm in Carrigan's tone.

I told them everything, from how Zander had died to how Kesta had shared that I was to be a savior for all of Aspasia. I also told them exactly what had happened the day of the attack, and about Kallisto's addition to the story—that my exploding like that was rare and due to a blip in my entranx pattern that wouldn't happen again. I then told them how I had realized an error in Kallisto's story about Zander through my dream.

"And what was the error?" Calix asked.

I explained that the dark phoenix had separated Zander from his body when the phoenix tried to kill him, so Zander couldn't have left the note at Uncle William and Aunt Maggie's house asking me to leave Earth. I told them how Kallisto had treated Taurik to make it look like he was someone I needed to avoid.

"I attempted to keep Kallisto and Kesta off my trail by pretending to be mad at Taurik and by being discreet with Professor Omega because I thought he knew something important that he wasn't saying." I left out the part about Meda contacting me via personal note on my first day. She had told me to keep that a secret, and I felt like disobeying her was not something anyone should do.

By the end of my story, Calix and Carrigan were both staring at me. Neither had sipped their drinks nor taken a bite of food. Calix opened his mouth as if he was about to say something but changed his mind and closed it again. Carrigan's expression had never changed from the time I started my story to its end.

"I know it's a lot to take in," I said.

Calix nodded. Part of me wondered if I had done the right thing in telling them everything. I hoped that they would still want to be my friends.

"You don't trust the headmistress?" Carrigan asked.

"Well, no, not really," I said. "There's something off about her."

"I see," he said slowly. "So you're basing all of your distrust for her on a *dream*?" The way he said it made it sound foolish on my part.

"Yes, I am."

"What if your memory of the dream is wrong?"

"I don't think it is."

"But what if it is?" He peered at me intently.

"Carrigan, I *know* I remembered the dream properly. As soon as I saw it in my mind, I knew without a doubt exactly what the dark phoenix had done. The images were so vivid, so real."

"Okay."

Calix spoke up. “Loddy, you said that this Zander called you a *quizeen*?"

"Yes."

"Are you aware that a quizeen is—”

"—a ruler over a quasian? Yes. Kesta told me."

"Quizeens are also referred to as princesses in some parts of the galaxy. What do you think possessed him to call you a quizeen?"

"Kesta said that she thought quizeen was Zander’s code name for me. She told me she thought he was a liphon, but I doubt that’s true."

Calix shook his head. “I don't know what to think.”

No one spoke for an entire minute. To diminish the feeling of awkwardness, I sipped a very long drink from my Pinkest Pucker while Calix mulled over the facts and Carrigan stared at his food.

Finally Calix spoke. "I still don't trust Taurik, though.”

"Ugh. Why not?" I asked.

"Even if he does seem to be against the headmistress, for all we know, his behavior could be an act. I am not saying that I distrust the headmistress, but Taurik could be in cahoots with her and be plotting against you. Or, if Kallisto is actually trying to help you out, Taurik could be trying to hurt both of you."

"Calix.” I sighed. I was becoming frustrated over hearing Taurik discussed as if he were this villain out to get me.

"Loddy, it just makes me uneasy that he’s a morbid,” Calix said.

"So what?" I could feel myself getting up from the table as the anger welled inside me. I had had enough. "I need to get to class. I'll see you both later. And until then, please keep this to yourselves."

"Of course." Calix nodded while Carrigan continued to stare at his food.

5

INCEPTION

During Quintessence, Professor Biv continued our discussion over the different structures an In-betweener's entranx pattern can take. He used the god Deo as an example of an In-betweener, just as Kesta had on my first day at Abervania. Over the past week, I'd realized just how big a deal this guy was. Not only was Deo discussed in Quintessence and History of Aspasia, but he had been discussed in every other class I had.

Since discussing Deo as a child, my History of Aspasia class had progressed through his journey on Earth and how he had unlocked the power of transportation in the first person. Using this power, he and his brother, Prodrian, had been able to transport themselves to a new galaxy that they were able to essentially organize from the ground up with the help of the other gods. Prodrian then tried to take over the new galaxy, but Deo and the rest of the gods defeated him. In History of Aspasia we also discussed the other gods and goddesses and how each had a unique personality. I thought it would have been exhilarating to meet them all despite the disparaging stories Kallisto and Kesta told about them.

The brains, as Kallisto called them, were Cato, Meda, and Amoura. They wrote the laws that laid the foundation for all of Aspasia's government. Under the laws, the Aspasian Empire had ten gods, as people called them, and each was to represent one of the ten power-types: Mind, Chaste, Air, Fire, In-between, Personality, Earth, Electricity, Aphotic, and Water. The gods' actual titles were *aspar* for men and *aspara* for women. They were all couples except for Amoura, and they all lived in one of the seven quasians or continents of Aspasia, but they made decisions regarding the whole of Aspasia. Their children, the quiziars and quizeens, ruled the quasians.

Under the quiziars and the quizeens were vitos and vitas who ruled over the individual vitars or countries. Under them were the zylars and zyleens who ruled over the zylos, or states. Under them were the zotiats and zoteens who ruled over the zots, or districts. Finally, under the zotiats and zoteens were the propiars and propeens who ruled over the prips or cities. It was all confusing, but I was glad I had an idea of how the government functioned. Abervania, the school, was located in the prip of Vashia.

The History of Aspasia professor, Yttira, told us that not one of the gods had resigned since taking office at the beginning of Aspasia approximately 3,700 years ago, or 370 Earth years. One would think that extreme corruption would have blossomed during those centuries, but it had not. Yttira confided that the gods had a secret in combating their own corruption, but he would not tell us what—or who— it was.

Cato, who represented the mind power-type, was the unofficial leader of the three Brains, but he never flaunted it. He had super-aspasian intelligence; he could concentrate on vast amounts of knowledge and understand any type of technology. He also possessed the ability to manipulate people's minds, but from what I had been taught, he had never done that.

Meda, who represented the chaste power-type, was said to be the least mellow of the three and brilliant. She, too, possessed super-aspasian intelligence and was a telepathist—she could read minds. She had reached peak aspasian potential, which meant that her body was at the acme of health and always would be, even if she never exercised again. I would have loved to have possessed peak aspasian potential.

Amoura, who represented the air power-type, was the Brain who no one could figure out. She was said to always keep to herself. People hadn't figured out if her preference for solitude was due to arrogance or to an inability to humor anyone who wasn't as brilliant as she. Amoura possessed superhuman intelligence, but she also possessed Innate Capability, which meant that she could understand any concept without having to invest time in learning it.

I remembered Kesta's telling me that Amoura was responsible for inventing Amourite, the brain-stimulating element which gave all Aspasians perfect recall. This meant that books did not have to be used in schools because, once the students heard the information from the instructor, they never forgot it.

Deo represented the in-between power-type; his wife Rhaine represented the personality power-type. Alexander, with whom he was at war, represented the fire power-type. The others were Balboq, who represented earth; Venexa, electricity; Stimheit, aphotology; and Timben, water.

Today when I walked into the History of Aspasia classroom, for the first time no scene was prepared for us to look upon while we listened to the lecture. I walked up to Carrigan who didn't acknowledge me, but I wasn’t surprised. We both waited for Yttira to start talking. He was present, but not in the way any of the students were because Yttira was the room.

"Today we are going to discuss a most interesting topic," Yttira began. "Have any of you ever heard of a phoenix?" My ears perked up, and I was startled to see that Carrigan’s had, too.

At this point, Melee—with unwavering confidence—would have begun explaining exactly what a phoenix was, but since the attack, she had transferred out of all the classes she had with me. She may have transferred because she was afraid of me like the other students, but part of me suspected it was an attention thing, too.

No one answered, so Yttira proceeded to explain that a phoenix was a spirit composed of emotions.

"Of course, not everyone can host a phoenix spirit. The phoenixes themselves are only meant to be merged with phoenix-holders—those who are destined to hold a phoenix spirit inside them. From an early age, phoenix-holders are systematically exposed to phoenixes until one happens to merge with him or her."

Someone raised a hand.

"Yes?" Yttira asked.

"Sir," the boy said, "are phoenix-holders confined to certain families such as those who routinely host phoenixes?"

"Like the Flares?"

"Yes, sir."

"Well, the Flares are all descended from the god Alexander Flare. He is a phoenix-holder as are all of his children and his wife. That, however, does not mean that every person born in that family will be a phoenix-holder. They all thus far just happen to have been blessed in that manner. Who is to say that Alexander and Pheona could have a child without that ability? It is possible.

"But back to your question. Are all phoenix-holders confined within certain families? No. Anyone can be a phoenix-holder provided he or she is blessed with that particular entranx energy. Why am I discussing phoenix spirits? Because it was through phoenix spirits that Prodrian Clevist attempted to take over all of Aspasia. Oddly enough, he was not a phoenix-holder."

"How was this possible, Yttira?" He had piqued my interest as he always did.

"Because he abused the power of the phoenixes. He perverted them to the point at which they were no longer in their pure forms."

Yttira was creating a scene for us. I watched the room begin to change as our surroundings transformed into a spacious, beautiful room like one would see in a palace. The large windows covered in red silk curtains on the right side of the room were twice my height. No light shone behind them, so I assumed it was nighttime. Before us was a humongous bed of intricately-molded cast-iron, covered with a red and gold comforter with intricate designs. Expensive furniture was positioned around the room.

The scene was frozen. Two men stood talking to one other. Actually, they looked like they were arguing; the red-faced man with gingerbread hair was open-mouthed as if he was yelling at the other man. He was leaning toward him with his finger extended as if making a point. The other man had charcoal hair. He looked amused, as if he thought the first man was making an absolute fool of himself.

"Do you recognize these two men, Loddy?" Yttira asked.

I looked more closely, but I did not recognize them. I stared again and realized that I did recognize them. The last time I had seen the two men, they were not men at all. They were little boys. "It's Deo and Prodrian, isn't it?"

"Yes. They look different now, don't they?"

"Yes, sir." They were taller and more muscular than they had been on Earth. They had also lost all of their baby fat and their features were chiseled. But once past the initial differences, I could see the glimmer of innocence in their little-boy eyes.

"I am going to allow the scene to play now so that you may all see what happened at this integral point in our history." Yttira unfroze the scene.

Deo spoke resolutely, his voice powerful and confident. "Prodrian, we know what you are trying to do."

"And what would that be, Brother?" Prodrian's voice, always on the edge of hissing, sounded like it should have come from the mouth of a snake.

"You want to overthrow all of us so that *you* can be emperor!" Deo yelled.

Prodrian laughed as if the thought of his taking over hadn't occurred to him.

"Admit it! We know that's what you're trying to do! You can't hide it anymore. Meda knows all about your secret operation with all those phoenixes. It's cruel, Prodrian—separating phoenix spirits from their holders just so you can add them to your own experimental phoenix!"

Prodrian's smile set. "Brother, how would any of you even know about an experimental phoenix? I doubt any of you have even seen it. Am I right?"

"That *was* true—until just a few moments ago," Deo said, taking a stab at his armor of indifference.

Prodrian's face lost all hint of relaxation. "What do you mean?" he demanded.

Deo walked away from his brother toward the window closest to them. Deo's expression was now the relaxed one. "I mean that one of my Aspasiars has actually seen the thing."

Prodrian's jaw locked.

"We received Intel about the experimental phoenix a few days ago, so I sent a team down to the prip where we heard the phoenix supposedly was. No one had seen anything—that is, up until now." He looked Prodrian straight in the eye. "You're pathetic, Prodrian."

Prodrian stared his brother down. Without warning he jumped at Deo and forced him to the ground. With his knees, he pinned both of Deo's arms, one on either side of his head. He then put his hands around his neck and squeezed. Deo was able to shove him off. He stood looking down at Prodrian, shaking his head.

"You could have done so much good for this place! Instead, you only look out for yourself."

Prodrian leaped up, hatred flashing in his eyes. "You're right! I *could* have done a lot of good for this place. But it's hard when your brother is the most powerful man in the galaxy, and his cronies are monitoring your every move!"

Deo paused to process his brother's words. He stepped toward Prodrian so that he was only an inch from his face. "*You-are-too-dangerous-not-to-be-monitored.*"

Prodrian smiled. "The same can be said for you, Brother."

The scene froze, with both men staring at each other with hatred.

"Shortly after," Yttira continued, "Prodrian escapes from the home where both men were during the scene, and Prodrian attempts to take over Aspasia. Why do you think this moment is so important in our history?"

"Because this is the moment the tide turned for both sides, right?"

"Exactly, Miss Clementine. This was the moment all pleasantries were pushed aside and the brothers declared war against one another." He sighed. "Now, I want all of you to focus on a particular point Deo made. He said that Prodrian stole phoenix spirits from their holders in order to make an experimental phoenix spirit. Exactly how did he do this?"

No one said anything.

"He did what no one should ever have the right to do. His aphotic cronies ripped phoenix spirits out of people's bodies using a technique called plyxing. Plyxing enables aphotics to cut any section of an entranx pattern they want. They can then destroy the section completely or paste it into another's entranx pattern. In Prodrian's case, they pasted the plyxed parts into his experimental phoenix's entranx pattern, thereby transferring every stolen phoenix spirit into the almighty phoenix. His cronies had stuffed almost 2,000 spirits into it before it was ripped out of Prodrian's body in the end."

"How was he able to merge with the almighty phoenix spirit once it had all of the other incompatible spirits inside it?" Carrigan asked.

"He warped his entranx pattern with aphotic energy."

"Let me get this straight," Carrigan said. "Using aphotic energy, Prodrian ripped phoenix spirits from other people's bodies, then stuffed these stolen spirits into the almighty phoenix's body, after which he used more aphotic energy to stuff the almighty phoenix into his own body?"

"Yes," Yttira said, "and since phoenix spirits live off the emotions of their holder, he was able to infuse almost 2,000 phoenixes with every dark emotion while he controlled their power. This made for the most dangerous, least stable force this galaxy has ever witnessed. Hopefully, no one will ever witness it again."

6

MEETING WITH THE HEADMISTRESS

I cornered Professor Zazz after Aspasian Technology. "Please, Professor, I need my appenda-port."

"I will return your appenda-port zoon, Mizz Clementine," he said. "But in the meantime, you should feel humbled by your contribution to Azpazian zcienze."

I huffed, but he didn't hear me. "Of course."

Later, as I entered the consummation hall, Kesta stopped me.

"Loddy!"

"Hey!"

"Headmistress Tempest wants to speak with you after you're done with classes for the day." Kesta's enthusiasm seemed more forced than usual. Her lilac eyes were not as relaxed as usual, either.

"Really? Over what?" I was curious, though I had some ideas concerning the meeting topics.

"Oh, I can't say. I'm just the messenger. How are your classes going?"

"Great! Professor Zazz still won't let me use my appenda-port." I rolled my eyes.

"That doesn't surprise me. The faculty is tired of hearing about your appenda-port. It's all he talks about whenever he's around anyone."

I raised my eyebrows in surprise.

"Hopefully he will give the appenda-port back to you soon, and we won't have to hear any more about it. If he doesn't, come to us," she said.

By *us*, I knew she was talking about herself and Kallisto.

"Of course. I doubt it will come to that," I said.

"You never know. Well, I must go. Don't forget to meet the headmistress in her office as soon as you're done with classes. Talk to you later!" She gave me a side-hug and whisked off.

After grabbing a bite, I found Taurik in aphotology and told him that I was going to be late for our project session.

"Why?"

"Kallisto wants to meet with me."

As soon as I said her name, his features tensed, but since a canceller was watching, I knew he wouldn't make a fuss.

"I see. Well, I guess I'll just wait for you."

"You don't have to do that." I forced myself to sound indifferent, but I was flattered that he would wait for me.

"I don't mind." He pierced me with those beautiful salmon eyes.

I wanted to let his eyes envelop me, but I reminded myself that a canceller was watching. "Well," I answered hastily, "if you're that eager to start the project, you can meet me outside the administration building after I finish speaking with Kallisto. I shouldn't be too long."

After my last class, I raced to Kallisto's office, wondering what she wanted to discuss. She wasn't the type to schedule a meeting for chit-chat. Something had to be important for her to request a specific meeting.

Kallisto looked up without changing her apathetic expression. Her chiseled features and crimson pantsuit made her even more intimidating.

"Hello, Loddy." Her voice was neutral—not cold, but not friendly, either.

"Hello, Headmistress."

Statues, contorted in abstract shapes, were positioned around the office, and a bookshelf adorned with untouched volumes stood to my side. She watched as I walked past the grey cancellers toward her desk. This time, I made out Pilmus from all the others. I almost waved to him, but decided against it since Kallisto was watching. When I sat down, the eerie flames on either side of her blazed full-force. As far as I knew, Kallisto was the one who had created them.

"How are your classes going?" she asked.

"They're going well. I love all of my professors. They're much different from the ones on Earth."

"In what way?"

"Well, the professors here aren't bound by reality. They don't spend all of their time indoctrinating us with theories. They spend their time encouraging us to think in ways that aren't hindered by the impossible because we aren't hindered by the impossible like people on Earth."

"Yes. So true." The headmistress nodded, then

paused. "The reason I have invited you here is to discuss Evily. I am sure you are wondering why I haven't assigned her to you?"

"Yes." My jaw set. As if I needed another reason to be mad at her. Why had she waited so long to tell me?

"Loddy, I've been pondering about her as your safeguard against the dark phoenix. If you aren't comfortable around Evily, I would rather she not be around you every second of the day."

What? Is Kallisto actually taking my *feelings into consideration?* A week ago she seemed adamant that Evily be with me at all times.

"Headmistress, I'll be fine. I was just whining when we talked about it earlier. I know how important it is for me to stay stable."

"No, Loddy, I can't put you through that."

"If you say so." To be honest, I was relieved that I didn't have to deal with Evily. Still, shadowing me would have forced Evily to communicate with me.

"Now that we have that out of the way, we must settle on a time to train you to mentally combat the phoenix. How about at this time every other day?"

"That will work."

"Good. Make sure you wear something suitable. Skirts won't do for hand-to-hand combat."

"Yes, ma'am."

"You should also work on the formations I will show you in your power practice sessions. I'm sure Professor Pex won't mind. By the way, how *is* power practice going?"

"Not well."

Her face remained neutral. I figured she already knew as much before she asked. Not much went on at Abervania that she didn't know.

"Really." She didn't even try to sound surprised.

"Yes. I'm still trying to adjust. I'm sure it will get better."

"Of course." She got up and moved to one of the windows overlooking the campus. "Tell me, Loddy. Is Evily in power practice with you?"

"Yes. Why?"

She continued to stare out the window. "I was just wondering."

I suspected there was more to her curiosity than she was telling me. I decided not to press the point because I needed to stay in her good graces.

She turned and gave me a humorless smile. "Is there anything you want to discuss before I talk with you about—about a certain someone?"

Now who could she be talking about, I thought sarcastically. However, there was something I wanted to ask first.

"There is."

Her eyebrows raised. "What is it?"

"Professor Omega. When is he going to be back?" I watched her control her facials as she processed my question as adroitly as if she weren't hiding anything from me.

"I don't know. He isn't feeling well at all."

"What's wrong with him?"

"As I told your class, he isn't feeling like himself."

So you are going to stick to your guns. "That could mean a lot of things. Is he sick?"

"Yes." Her voice was resolute.

"What's causing his illness?" I couldn't wait to hear what she said.

"I can't say."

"Why not?"

"Because I am afraid it is more serious than we thought."

Oh, no. "He isn't dying, is he?"

Kallisto stared at me then she returned to her desk. She paused as if she was choosing her words carefully before looking up. "I am not sure. We are communicating with him daily, though. If anything happens, we will know."

Professor Omega knows something. He must for them to have completely removed him from campus. "He isn't at home?"

"No," she replied.

"Is there any way I could see him?"

"I would rather you not until we figure out what's wrong with him."

Big surprise. I wanted to sigh in frustration, but controlled myself to appear neutral. If Kallisto sensed how much I wanted to talk with Professor Omega, she might have realized that I suspected more than she thought.

"Okay."

"Please understand, Loddy. There's nothing I can do about it."

“I see. I guess I’ll meet with Professor Omega when he gets back.” I smiled at her innocently despite my true feelings: I *would* talk to Professor Omega, and I *would* find out what he knew about my past—even if that meant rescuing him from Kallisto herself.

“Yes.”

Kallisto was suppressing the smugness in her voice, implying that she had no plans to allow Professor Omega on campus anytime soon.

“Now, about that certain someone—” she began.

“Headmistress,” I interrupted. I had already formulated my argument in my mind, an argument that didn’t place blame on Taurik, myself, or anyone else in the class. “I knew you didn’t want me around Taurik, but I couldn’t help it. We were the last two people in the class without partners. We didn’t have any choice.” After all, Taurik and I *had* technically been the last two people in the room without a partner after Bite and Jazda were assigned to one another.

Kallisto stared at me. “You didn’t try to partner with anyone else?” she asked. The flames on either side of her desk flickered. She was becoming angry.

“It all happened so fast. As I told you, I’m still trying to adjust to my new environment.”

Another small flicker. She continued staring at me without blinking. “I see. And there isn’t any way you can be with someone else at this point?”

I tried to sound disappointed. “No, we have already started the project. Switching partners now would only put me further behind.”

She pursed her lips. "Then it seems we can't do anything about this now."

I shook my head.

"But there *is* something we can do about the venue where you and he conduct your project."

Great. She had heard about Taurik's being inside Chaste Palez. "You know about that?"

"Of course I know. And I am displeased with you, Loddy. How could you willingly have let him into your *own* palez?" As anger rose in her voice, the flames flickered more intensely.

"We couldn't find a quiet place."

Flicker. "You could have gone to the library."

"I didn't know where it was."

Flicker. "You could have asked *him* where it was." She made Taurik sound as if he were a lowly dog instead of a human.

I had to admit I was enjoying myself even though she could have blown a gasket at any moment. "Asking Taurik never occured to me." The red in her eyes became more pronounced. "I know you don't like him," I added.

"And I believe I have provided you with ample evidence as to why I feel the way I do!" The flames flared more than I had ever seen them, growing to twice the size they had been, but I didn't flinch.

"You did," I said calmly, "but I had no choice. That Taurik makes you so nervous makes me wonder if he is knows something that you don't want me to know."

The flames shrank and the red in her eyes lost its vibrancy. "It's not that," she said hastily, struggling to hide the nervousness that was attempting to overtake her.

"So it's just that he steals memories?"

"Yes." She forced herself to stare back at me.

"I *will* be careful."

"I am afraid that will not be good enough."

"That is all that I can offer you right now."

Flicker. She leaned in toward me until her face was only a few inches from mine. "I hope you know that you have placed Kesta and me in a very uncomfortable position by being Taurik's partner."

"I'm sorry. I can only assure you that it was not intentional." But it was.

She leaned back and regarded me with utter disgust. "Your apology changes nothing. I don't want him in Chaste Palez." She stood. "We will meet in the power practice gym for lessons. You may go."

I got up so fast that I wondered if my body was acting on its own. I hurried out of her office without risking a glance back, which would only have made matters worse.

The moment I left Kallisto's office, I knew three things to be true: first, I had the knowledge to make even Kallisto squirm; second, I would use that knowledge to expose her for who she really was—a downright scoundrel; and third, that whether Kallisto knew it or not, she and I were waging a battle for the truth—a battle that had only just begun.

7

PLANESIAN PEVDOTS

As soon as I walked out of the administration building, I saw Taurik leaning against the wall watching the world around him as if it were all new. When he noticed me looking at him, he smiled and joined me.

My heart beat as hard as it used to whenever Zander looked at me. Apart from Taurik's chiseled cheek bones, I couldn't help but stare at his muscular arms and chest. As usual, the black shirt he was wearing outlined his pecs . . .

Before he could notice my staring, I shifted my eyes to his face. He was still smiling. "So, what did the dragon lady have to say?"

"She's furious that we're partners in aphotology."

His smile broadened. "Good."

"She doesn't want us meeting in Chaste Palez anymore."

"Of course she doesn't. Which is all the more reason to do it."

"Taurik, I really don't think we should test her any further. Why are you so comfortable disobeying her, anyway? Everyone else is too afraid to even look at her the wrong way."

"Let's just say I have insurance."

"Insurance? What does that mean?"

He looked around as if expecting to see someone watching us. His instincts were probably right since someone was watching me at all seconds of the day anyway. "Let's get out of here, and I can tell you more. Where do you want to go?"

The perfect place hit me. I was surprised I hadn't thought of it sooner. "How about the Pinkest Pokest?" As soon as I'd said it, I realized it might have sounded like I was forcing him on a date.

"Sure."

Did he just agree to a date? I stifled my enthusiasm at this possibility.

At the Pinkest Pokest, one of the many waiters with runes across his face greeted us at the door. Smiling, he asked Taurik, "Do you have a table preference?"

Then I saw something that I had never seen. Taurik Night looked uneasy as he processed what the waiter had asked him.

"Uh, no, not at all," Taurik said.

I could hear nervousness in his voice that was different from the usual confidence that rang through it.

The waiter led us to a secluded table near the back of the eatery, gave us our menus, and bustled off. Taurik looked around as if he were in the middle of his worst nightmare.

"Are you okay?" I asked. He looked at me as if realizing for the first time since entering the eatery that I was there. He tried to mask his uneasiness, but I could tell he was challenged.

"Yeah, of course. What's good here?"

"You are not okay. What's wrong?" And then it occurred to me that he was afraid to be seen with me.

He looked around again before resuming eye contact with me. "I haven't been to this eatery. It's just—different."

Ahh, of course. Taurik was an aphotic, and I had picked an eatery geared toward chastes. He was out of his element. "Taurik, I am so sorry."

Mr. Barboo appeared behind Taurik and smiled. "Ah, Miss Clementine."

I hadn't noticed him approach our table. When Mr. Barboo turned to Taurik, his smile disappeared.

"Oh, Taurik Night." He stiffened. "How are you?"

Taurik looked him over, and that calm, reassured look returned. He stared into Mr. Barboo's eyes. "I am well, sir, thank you. I don't think we have met, though." He stood and extended his hand.

Mr. Barboo took his hand reluctantly. "Mr. Barboo. Nice to finally meet you, Taurik Night. I have heard—"

"—horrible things about me, I'm sure." Taurik smiled. He sat and waited as Mr. Barboo tried to find a civil counter to his blunt surmise.

Mr. Barboo didn't come up with anything, so he just let out a hearty, though somewhat fake, laugh before shifting his attention back to me. "What are you, a chaste, doing with an illustrious morbid like Taurik?" His voice was tinged with that ever-present desire for news.

"We are working on a project for aphotology. We have to ask each other one hundred questions to get to know each other better."

The interest in his eyes grew. I knew what he was thinking: Why was I doing the project with Taurik of all people?

"I see. And you both picked each other to be partners?" I knew it.

"Yes, sir!" Taurik spoke through clenched teeth. "I snapped her up before anyone else could get her! Do you blame me?" Taurik and Mr. Barboo looked at each other, and I could tell that Mr. Barboo was completely taken aback by Taurik's lack of subtlety. He opened his mouth to answer, then closed it and turned to me in surprise.

"No, of course not," Mr. Barboo finally said. He tried to regain control of the conversation. "Has anyone taken your drink orders?"

"No, they haven't," I said.

"What would you like?"

"I'll take a Pinkest Pucker. Taurik, what do you want?"

"Do you have Bottomless Pits?" Taurik asked.

"Eh, no. We don't make those here."

"Of course you don't. I'll just have water."

Then Mr. Barboo was gone. I was sure he would not be the one to bring our drinks to avoid seeing Taurik again.

"Taurik, please be kind. He's a very pleasant man."

"I'm sure he is. He just doesn't like me." He began to scan his menu.

"He doesn't understand you."

"That's the story of my life."

"Speaking of the story of your life, are you going to

tell me about your insurance policy?"

He looked up. "Maybe—if you tell me what's good here."

"I haven't ever eaten here. I only come for drinks." I looked down at my menu to find something that looked familiar. "I have no idea what any of this is."

He scanned some more. "Wait. Here's something," he said, pointing to the menu.

I leaned over to see what he was talking about.

"Planesian Pevdots. I've heard they're delicious."

I shrugged. "Works for me. Just as long as they're edible."

A different waiter appeared and served our drinks. As he reached to give me my drink, I noticed the runes all the way down his arm.

"Are you ready to order?" he asked in a resonating bass.

I looked at Taurik who extended his hand to convey that I could order first. "I'd like the Planesian Pevdots."

"I'd like the same," Taurik said.

The waiter nodded and took our menus. "I will get that order in. Let me know if you need anything."

Taurik resumed looking around. I knew he was trying to put off telling me about his insurance policy.

"Taurik?"

"Yes?" Then he noticed my Pinkest Pucker, and by his eager look, I knew he was going to use it to put off telling me his secret.

"What did you call that thing?"

"A Pinkest Pucker."

"That looks a lot better than my water. Could I try it?"

"I'd let you, but it has some odd side effects."

"Like what?"

"It has femino essence—"

"—so I might start acting like you after a few sips?"

"Probably." I giggled. "That would be funny to watch, though."

His eyes enlarged in mock surprise. "Really? And why would that be so funny?"

"Because—" I paused. "Because you always act so cool and standoffish."

He smiled broadly. "Do I?"

"Yes, you do." I sipped my Pinkest Pucker. As usual, the fizz made my mouth tingle.

"If you want, I can act less cool and standoffish."

"No, no. Don't change who you are. I like the way you are."

The eager look swam into his eyes. "Really? Are you sure about that? You don't know anything about me."

"I know you're a good person, and that's enough for me."

The eager look left his eyes and was replaced by a sad one. "Oh, Loddy. I am *very* far from a good person."

"No, you aren't."

He looked down at the table, cradling his forehead and shaking his head from side to side.

"Taurik, you have a genuine heart. I can tell."

He shook his head more vigorously. "No, no, no. I don't. I *really* don't. If only you knew."

"Then tell me. Why don't you have a genuine heart?"

"I can't."

"Because you're a morbid?"

"Yes."

"And I'm guessing you can't tell me about your insurance policy either, can you?"

He looked up at me with genuine sadness in his eyes. "No."

"Taurik, I—"

"Loddy, I know it's irritating being in the dark. But I assure you, you will find the truth once you uncover Kallisto's secrets. That's all I can say at the moment."

"Why did you lie and say you were going to tell me about your insurance policy when you knew that you couldn't?"

"That's all I could think of. I was afraid Kallisto was listening in on us, and I wanted to get away as soon as possible. And—"

"And?" His eyes were so intense that my heart beat faster.

"And . . ." He continued staring at me as if he was going to say something important.

"Yes?"

"And that's it."

My heart slumped. "I see. So let me get this straight: You can hover secrets in front of me for leverage, but when it comes to *telling* those secrets, you can get out of telling me by using your morbid excuse that you'll die if you tell a secret. I can't complain because if you tell me a secret, I'll lose you. You always have the upper hand."

"When you put it that way—"

"Everything pertains to *you*!"

"It's more complicated than that."

He was driving me insane. I couldn't get any secrets out of him, and I couldn't do anything about it. I didn't want him to stay a complete mystery forever.

"Loddy, I know it doesn't seem fair, but you're just going to have to trust me, okay?"

He gazed at me, and I knew then that I would have to trust him for our relationship to work. I nodded.

The waiter arrived with our food. I looked down to see one hundred transparent tadpole eggs. Instead of multi-colored organisms, these clear "eggs" held red organisms rolled up in a ball like tadpoles. Tiny, black eyes jutted out of the sides of each head.

I looked over at Taurik. He was struggling to contain his disgust. My stomach roiled as well, but I managed to keep my face neutral while the waiter hovered.

"Do you need anything else? Refills?" the waiter asked.

We shook our heads.

"Okay. Enjoy!"

I looked back at Taurik who had begun picking at the eggs as if they held poisonous snakes instead of something edible.

"Is this for real?" he asked.

"I think so."

"I'm not eating this. I don't care *how* delicious people think it is." He threw his fork down and pushed his plate away. "Sorry about that, Loddy. I'll get the visuals next time I recommend food for you, okay?"

I giggled. "Okay."

"So," he said pulling his bilbop out of his pocket, "Do you want to answer some questions or are you going to try one of those things?"

I looked down at the pevdots and considered being open-minded, but as I looked more closely, I saw how slimy they were. *Ugh.* I pushed my plate away. "Maybe some other time," I said.

"Or never, right?"

I giggled. "Or never."

He laughed, and we locked eyes at the same time. He held my gaze, not wanting to drop it.

"So I guess you're ready to start?"

"Sure."

The folder of papers materialized in front of him. He undid the clasp and examined the questions we had answered so far. "We're on question eleven. In other words, we still have a long way to go."

"Okay."

"Question eleven: *What type of aphotic powers does your partner possess?*" He looked at me expecting an answer.

I didn't know what to say.

"Do you want me to just write 'Possessed by an evil spirit'?"

"No, we can't do that." The sad part about it was that he was on point with his statement.

"Why not? It's true."

"I don't want to word the response that way."

"Why not?"

"Because I don't want to bring more attention to the truth."

"Fine. How would you suggest I word the answer?"

I thought for a few moments, trying to figure out how to describe my power without making it sound like I was a bloodthirsty murderer. "I know. Unknown. You could just write that I am still trying to figure out my powers—which I am."

His disappointed look said everything about my answer.

"What?"

"It sounds like you're dodging the question."

"It is the truth."

He rolled his eyes. "I'm just going to write that you possess a little of all the aphotic powers."

I remembered when Kesta told me the same thing after our first meeting on Earth. At the time, I had no idea what she meant. But now, I realized that that was the perfect description for my power.

"Fine. What about you?" I asked.

"You already know what powers I have."

"I do?"

"Yes. Don't tell me you've forgotten."

I knew that he could steal memories at will, but I wondered if I could get anything else out of him. "Of course I haven't forgotten, but it's your answer. You need to state your powers."

"Ugh."

"You're a very pleasant person. It's somewhat hard for me to wrap my mind around the fact that you do what you do."

"Well, I do what I have to do."

"I know you do. You haven't taken any of my memories, have you?"

"Of course not. I wouldn't ever do that to you—although Kallisto probably told you otherwise."

"Don't worry. I don't believe a word she says. How do you steal people's memories, anyway? Do you just take a random person's, or do you exact revenge on people who mistreat you?"

"Eh, a little of both."

"Taurik! That's horrible!"

"What? You asked, and I gave you an honest answer."

The waiter with the runes down his arm returned. As he refilled my drink, he tried to appear nonchalant about whether we'd tried our food.

"Do we not like the pevdots?" he asked.

"Have you *seen* them?" Taurik asked.

"Yes, sir, plenty of times. It's one of our most popular dishes." He filled Taurik's glass without looking at him.

"Really." Taurik made no attempt to conceal his sarcasm.

He looked Taurik straight in the eye. "Really."

"Then may I ask what exactly a pevdot is?"

"It's an egg from the paltakeet in the northern quasian of Planesia."

Taurik sized the waiter up as he spoke, and I noticed for the first time that the waiter was handsome. He had a perfect tan complexion and caramel curls. He was also muscular like Taurik.

"What's your name?" Taurik asked.

"Benter." He turned to me. "Do you need anything else, miss?"

"No, thank you—Benter."

He turned back to Taurik. "Does the gentleman require anything else?"

Taurik looked like he was wracking his brain for something clever to say, and for a moment it looked like he might, but then thought better of it. "Not that I know of."

"I will be back to check later. Don't hesitate to ask should you think of anything." This time as he walked away, Taurik watched him.

"Who is that guy?" he asked.

"I don't know. I have only seen him here."

"He's cocky."

"Taurik, he just answered your question."

"He thinks he's a big deal." He looked behind as if expecting to find Benter standing there, listening.

"Did you write down the description of your power yet?"

"Oh, no, but I will." He scribbled his answer and then read the next question to himself. "Wow. So the next question is, *What does your power say about you?*"

"I want *you* to answer this one first since I answered the last one first."

He sighed, frustrated. "Ugh, Loddy. I don't know."

"Yes, you do. Come on, Taurik. Just try."

He sighed again. Then with a rueful grin, he said, "Well, if I had to guess, I would say that my power says I feed off of other people's happiness. I say that because memories are used to build lives. In a way, they link all of us together. So when I steal a person's memories, it's like I'm stealing a part of that person, a part of that person's identity, a part of that person's life so that I can survive. I get what I need, but at what cost?"

He leaned closer. "After all, what is life without memories? It isn't life at all. It's an empty existence. In a way, every time I steal a memory from someone, I murder him a little bit more because I take a little more of his life with me."

I was speechless. I had never looked at memories that way, but he was right. Memories *did* form the basis of a meaningful life.

"Do you think that will work?" he asked nonchalantly.

"Sure."

"Good. Your turn."

Ugh. I hated talking about my power because it was so depressing. Of course, after hearing Taurik discuss his power, I realized I wasn't the only one who struggled accepting my abilities.

"Okay. Hmm . . . I would say that my power is, well, undefinable."

"Undefinable? That's basically what you said for the last question."

"Fine. Since my power takes on so many forms, that

must mean that I don't have a definite personality. You can't figure me out no matter how hard you try. Therefore, I am undefinable."

Taurik stared at me and raised his eyebrows in mock-surprise. "Not bad."

"Thank you."

"Next. *Do you feel like your life is headed in a positive direction?* It's your turn to answer first."

"I don't know."

"What do you mean, you don't know?"

"I mean, I have no idea if my life is headed in a positive direction. I don't know who to trust apart from you—you and I guess Calix and Carrigan."

"Who are they? Wait—are they the guys you eat with during consummation?"

"Yes."

"They seem off to me."

"Taurik!"

"What? They do."

"They're my friends."

"So? Just because they're your friends doesn't mean you shouldn't keep your guard up around them."

"They're *just fine*."

"Okay, if you say so." He smiled sarcastically. "Just answer the question, please."

"Fine. No, I don't feel like my life is going in a positive direction."

"Reason?"

"I feel clueless about everything."

"That's no reason to feel like your life isn't going in

a positive direction. Sometimes being clueless is bliss."

"What's wrong with Calix and Carrigan?"

He looked up from what he was writing to examine my expression, as if he was trying to figure out if I had meant to ask the question.

"I just said they felt off to me. That may or may not mean anything."

"But with you, it probably means something, right?"

"No. I'm just voicing my opinion. That's all. They may be perfectly innocent."

"*May* being the operative word?"

"No. *May* being the redeeming word. There's the possibility that I am completely wrong."

"Which is what I'm betting on." I reveled in my smart-alecky response. "Your turn, mister."

"I'll just write that I'm clueless, too." As he wrote, he popped a pevdot he'd been rolling around on the table into his mouth. He began to chew forgetting what he had said about them earlier.

Suddenly he stopped writing and froze.

I continued to smile at him. I was enjoying watching karma get the best of Mister Smarty-Pants.

He spat out the pevdot, grabbed the nearest napkin, and wiped his mouth in haste.

"What's the matter, Taurik? Don't like the pevdots as much as you thought you would?"

"No, it's worse."

"What do you mean?"

"I mean that cocky waiter was right about the stupid

things. They're delicious."

8

Complications

After sitting at the Pinkest Pokest for two hours, we finished all but five questions. We could have completed the questionnaire, but Taurik wanted to escape the cheery atmosphere that made him uncomfortable and Benter, the waiter with whom he had an issue. As we were leaving, I noticed Benter cleaning our table and grinning down at Taurik's empty plate.

We walked in silence until we reached Chaste Palez. We stopped but didn't look at each other. I felt guilty but couldn't figure out why.

"I'll see you tomorrow."

I nodded, but he didn't leave like I thought he would. I looked up into his beautiful salmon eyes and everything disappeared.

"Have you heard anything else about your appendaport?"

Of course he would ask that. "No. Professor Zazz—"

"—won't give it back." He sighed. "I guess you'll have to get ugly with him."

"Taurik! I can't get ugly with a *teacher*!"

"Why not?" He asked as if it were perfectly normal.

"Because he's a teacher! That's reason enough."

He rolled his eyes. "It's *your* appenda-port—"

"—that *he* helped me construct."

"But it's *yours*. He has no right to keep it from you if all the other students have theirs."

Taurik was right. "Well . . ."

"Well?"

"Maybe you're right."

"Of course I'm right." Mischief and unwavering confidence were in his eyes. He looked adorable.

"Good night, Taurik."

He opened his mouth for a comeback but smiled instead. "Good night, Loddy."

The next day during consummation, Daimon Chaser sat next to me. "Hey, Loddy! What's up?"

Calix, Carrigan, and I stopped talking and stared at him, his smile showcasing his perfectly white, symmetrical teeth.

"Not much, Daimon. What about with you?"

"I wanted to ask you something." His eyes teemed with curiosity. "Have you given any more thought to being on the duel team?"

"No, not really."

"I'm sure with the attack and having to adjust to a new school you haven't had time to think. But it'd be great if you'd consider it."

Being on the duel team would have been fun except I was a risk. If I lost control, I'd put everyone on the field in immediate danger.

"If you feel uncomfortable, we can be careful. I'm willing to do whatever it takes." The eagerness in his eyes was genuine.

"Could I sit in on a practice?"

His eyes dilated in excitement. "That's perfect! We practice today after school. Can you come?"

"Sure."

"Great! See you then! Bye, guys!"

I smiled half-heartedly at my friends. "I guess I'm on the duel team now?"

"Can you handle it?" Calix asked.

"Yeah, sure. You heard what he said. We can be careful."

"I don't know." Carrigan sounded doubtful, but of course he would be skeptical. He always was.

"Don't you think I can handle it?"

He wouldn't make eye contact. "I don't know. You could be asking for trouble."

"I want to at least try to be on the team. I can't let the phoenix prevent me from enjoying life, right?"

"Right!" Calix smiled half-heartedly, trying to look supportive.

After our last class that day, aphotology, Taurik pulled me aside.

"Come on. Let's go finish the questionnaire."

"I can't. I'm watching the duel team practice."

"The *duel team*?" His expression was one of surprise mixed with disgust. "*Why*?" "Because Daimon asked me to."

"That doesn't mean you have to."

"What if I want to, Taurik? Did you ever think of that?"

Disbelief registered in his eyes. "So you want to?"

"Yes."

He searched my face for weakness but found none. "I see. Have fun with that."

"I will." I held his gaze then walked away.

He waited before yelling, "The practice fields are the other way!"

Annoyed, I stopped and turned.

"Unless, of course, you're going the long way—"

I hated that he was right about everything. I was sure he was smiling smugly, but I refused to look.

"Do you want me to show you?"

Ugh. He was right again. I wasn't marching off in the wrong direction because I was distracted; I didn't know where the practice fields were. Still, if I hadn't been in a hurry, I would have refused his help and found someone to ask, or I would have searched for hours to keep him from having the satisfaction of besting me again. Still not looking at him, I nodded.

As we walked along he asked, "Are you sure you really want to do this?" His anxiety sounded genuine.

I nodded. He would have to work harder for conversation.

"Aren't you concerned about what could happen?"

I shook my head.

We walked through parts of the school I'd never seen because my classes were on the other side of campus.

"Will you at least tell me *why* you aren't concerned about what could happen?"

I wasn't going to crack.

"I think you're making a big mistake—"

I faced him head-on. "I can't let this rule my life, Taurik! I can't live inside a bubble!"

His features softened. "I just want you to be careful."

"*Be careful*? Look who's talking! You're on the headmistress's bad side all the time!"

"That's different."

"How?

"I don't put countless people's lives in danger when I take *my* risks."

He was so close that I could see the individual shades of salmon in his irises. "I don't put people's lives at risk, either." I closed in so we were as close as we could be without kissing. "I'm taking lessons."

"What if the lessons don't stop your outbursts?"

"If you're so worried, why don't you just join the team and monitor me yourself?" My senses were impaired by anger, so I didn't realize what I was saying.

"Because I'm afraid of hitting a pretty girl like you." I could see the desire in his eyes. He was going to kiss—

"*What is going on here*?" a familiar voice asked. The disgust in her voice was as clear from yards away as it would have been up close.

Kallisto stormed toward us, glaring.

"Nothing much. And with you?" Taurik's voice

didn't have a trace of fear.

She stared at him with more intensity than I had ever seen in her eyes. I almost thought I saw flames swimming in them. "I will ask my question again, and this time, I expect a direct answer. *What-is-going-on*?"

"He was showing me where the duel fields are."

She would not make eye contact with me as her eyes remained fixated on Taurik. "I see." The calmness in her voice was of the sort that scared me. "Did she ask for assistance, or did you force yourself into the situation?"

"I asked—"

She cut me off with her raised palm. She stepped toward Taurik and stared him down.

He stared back with as much if not more defiance.

"*Did-she-ask-you*?"

"No. I asked her."

Her face was as close to his as mine had been a moment earlier. "Mr. Night, I am going to tell you this for the last time: leave Miss Clementine *alone*."

The mischievous look in his eyes melted into pure anger. "And *I* am going to tell *you* one last time, *Headmistress*. I will *not* leave Loddy alone as long as she wants me around. And there is *nothing* you can do about it, so *stop trying*."

Flames appeared as the anger in her eyes intensified, and her hands glowed red. I thought she was going to kill him, but Taurik's gaze never faltered.

"*You-are-out-of-line, Mr. Night*." Kallisto spoke through clenched teeth.

"My actions are nothing compared to yours,

Headmistress." He stared at her intensely. "If you don't want her to know, leave us alone. I don't care to sacrifice a secret."

The fire disappeared from her eyes, and the glow faded from her hands.

"Come on, Loddy." He headed for the exit.

I stayed where I was. I wanted to go with Taurik, but I didn't want her to know that my allegiance was with him.

Her eyes still riveted on Taurik, Kallisto addressed me. "Go on. And don't forget about our session tomorrow."

I nodded. Without looking back, I left feeling as if something monumental and egregious had just happened.

9

DUEL PRACTICE

When the main building was far behind us, I said, "And you say *I'm* the reckless one?" Taurik burst out laughing. "You don't know how long I've been holding that in."

I was glad he was happy, but I was concerned for him. I had never seen Kallisto so mad. "You realize repercussions will follow?"

"Oh, yes. She's ticked off. I have no idea what she'll do."

"Taurik." I touched his shoulder and stared into his eyes. "I'm worried about you."

The giddiness in his eyes faltered, and hints of seriousness replaced them. "Why?"

"Because she's evil. We still don't know what she did to Professor Omega. He may not even—"

"Even what?"

"He may not even . . . be alive." I didn't want to consider that possibility.

"Loddy, I'm not afraid of her."

"I think that's where you're making a mistake."

"She can't do anything to me. If only you knew the terms of my insurance—"

"Even if you have the most fortified insurance plan,

she'll break the terms if you're in her way."

His eyes centered on me. "I don't think so."

"I do. Please be careful, Taurik. I don't want to lose you, too."

He dropped his gaze. "You'll be late for practice."

As we neared the transparent dome, I took in its massiveness. At the entrance, Taurik led me through glass doors.

"Old-fashioned automatic doors? I didn't think they existed here."

"Not everything operates via appenda-port, you know. Especially at a grobe."

"A grobe?"

"Yeah. That's what Aspasians call this building. It's the broad name for any massive athletic complex in Aspasia."

We walked into what looked to be a lobby. The furniture was unimpressive except for a futuristic control panel encased in a glass cubicle.

After walking through another set of double doors, Taurik led me through a passageway between two sets of high bleachers. The glass-enclosed dome was much larger on the inside and reminded me of the Colosseum. Soft, green turf covered its floor, and curved seats made of what looked to be titanium occupied the space around its outer rim. I figured in a galaxy that catered to the needs of its people, the seats would be softer than metal.

"What are the seats made of?"

"Laxon. It's very soft for Aspasian butts."

I giggled. Ahead, a group of people surrounded

Daimon, apparently laughing at a joke he had told. His whitewashed smile glimmered from yards away. Except for one fellow with bright red hair, I recognized the whole team. Massive but lovable Kabe was warming up and, unfortunately, so were Melee and Blaze. Melee flipped her laser-red hair as she spoke hurriedly to Blaze, who looked like a blonde Amazon. *Since Valisa isn't around, maybe they won't be so vicious.* Tiny Meena flitted about, as usual in the happiest of moods.

Daimon's eyes lit up when he saw me, but when he saw Taurik, his smile disappeared. He whispered to Kabe and the red-headed fellow, and in sync, the whole group stopped laughing and stared at Taurik.

Meena's was the only pleasant expression—although, with that dazed look in her turquoise eyes, she seemed more like she was ogling Taurik. Seeing her gaze at him that way solidified my resolve to lie to her about Taurik's and my relationship.

Taurik's gait never changed despite the group's expressions.

As we neared, Melee and Blaze glared at me. When Kabe and Meena saw me, they smiled and waved.

"Daimon." Taurik's eyes were calm and respectful.

"Taurik." Daimon's tone was calm. "Are you here to try out?"

"No. I just wanted to make sure Loddy was in the right hands."

Daimon grinned. "She's in the right hands, Taurik, I assure you."

Taurik stared at him. "Good." His eyes settled on

someone behind Daimon. "I guess I'll be going." He turned to me. Speaking like I was the only one there, he said, "I'll see you after practice."

I nodded.

He left, the whole group watching.

Daimon centered back on me with a wide smile. "Are you ready for your first practice?"

"I thought I was observing."

"If you don't mind, we need one more player to make the teams even."

"Um, yeah." I could hear the nervousness in my voice.

"Don't worry. You'll be fine. Do you know how a duel works?"

"Two people fight each other, right?"

"Yes. Two teams oppose each other. Each team must have the same number of players so that every person fights only one other opponent. Each pair fights in its own individual sector where no one else can interfere. Each duel continues until someone is knocked out, whereupon the opponent is the victor. To be deemed *knocked out*, the person has to be on the ground for at least ten seconds."

To think I would have to be violent was odd.

"The victors fight until one team is eliminated. Only two at a time fight. Make sense?"

"Yes."

"Do you know everyone?"

I figured everyone knew me after having seen my ugly side. If not, they had probably heard about me. I pointed to the red-head. "I don't know *him*."

"That's Resno!"

Resno waved. "And you are *the* Loddy. It's nice to meet you." Stretching out every word, he reminded me of a surfer dude.

"Likewise."

Daimon pulled me aside. "Resno is—kind of slow. He doesn't hurry, but he has a fascinating ability. He can absorb people's brain cells to render them as mentally dull as he is, slowing their processing and reaction times. When he absorbs their brain cells, he is temporarily smarter than they are."

"Really?"

"Yes. After a while, the additional brain cells cause him mental strain, so he has to give them back. He comes in handy on the field."

"I can imagine." I caught Kabe's eye.

"You know Kabe, right?"

"Yes. We have quintessence together."

"Whoa, Daimon. You should see her entranx pattern," Kabe said. "It's out of this world!" "I don't doubt it. Are you familiar with Kabe's abilities?"

I wracked my brain. "Confidi entranx?"

Kabe's smile intensified. "Right!"

Meena was hovering around our group. Making eye contact with me, she smiled.

"You know Meena?"

"We have power practice together."

"Great! You know Meena is an Encourager?"

"Yes."

"Great!"

The remaining teammates were practicing fight formations.

"And you know Melee and Blaze . . ." His tone suggested his knowledge of our relationship.

I nodded.

"Do you know their abilities?"

"Melee can make herself invisible?"

"Yes, but more specifically, she can bend light rays to create illusions."

"Right. I don't know Blaze's abilities."

"Super strength and flight."

"When he says super strength, he means it," Kabe added. "She could probably pick up the entire campus and fling it."

Wow, I thought. I should have known she was strong by her burly appearance. I turned to Daimon. "What do *you* do?"

Daimon grinned. "I possess peak human potential, which means I'm as fit as a human can be. I also have an energy reserve that increases with exhaustion."

"Backup energy?"

"Exactly! That second reserve of energy is more potent than the first, so I become a lightning bolt."

"Wow. So it's almost impossible to overcome that unlimited reserve of energy?"

He grinned self-consciously. "I guess you could say that."

He was more modest than his girlfriend.

"Do you have any other questions?"

"I don't think so."

"Then we'll get started." He assessed everyone and ordered, "Huddle up!"

Melee and Blaze sighed in annoyance.

"Take your time, girls. We aren't in a hurry." He was being sarcastic, but he was used to their bad attitudes.

Melee and Blaze remained outside of the huddle making a point not to come anywhere near me.

Standing in the center of the huddle, Daimon announced, "I'm excited Loddy is here today!"

Melee and Blaze snickered.

"As captain, I'm asking all of you to respect her out of respect for me. Do we have an understanding?"

Melee and Blaze rolled their eyes.

"Let's get started! Partner up, and whoever partners with Loddy, teach her our fight formations."

"I will!" Kabe said.

"Okay. I will assess everyone. Now go!"

After leading me away, Kabe asked, "What do you think?"

"What do I think?"

"Are you gonna join?"

"I want to."

"But are you going to?"

"I don't know." I shrugged. "We'll see."

"I know someone who would love to have you around." He grinned.

Attempting to keep him on task, I said, "Show me those fight formations, or Daimon may not let me come back."

"Nah, he wouldn't do that."

"Show me anyway."

He rolled his eyes. "I guess."

Kabe showed me the fight formations taking every opportunity to brush my arm or hand.

After we'd practiced for a while, Daimon appeared with an expectant expression. "What do you think, Loddy? Can you handle it?"

"Oh, yeah."

Daimon smiled. "Can you show me the formations?"

"Sure."

As Kabe and I demonstrated the formations we'd been practicing, Daimon watched, intent on my form.

"Not bad, Loddy."

"She catches on fast," Kabe said.

"That doesn't surprise me. What else can you do?"

"I don't know."

"You can control fire, can't you?"

Ugh. Please don't remind me. "Yeah . . ."

"How did you release that much power? From what the headmistress said, you weren't in the right state of mind. Have you ever controlled fire before?"

"No. I'm starting lessons with the headmistress tomorrow."

"Have you consciously used your abilities?" Daimon and Kabe were centered in.

"No."

"Are you serious?" they asked in unison, their eyes enlarged.

"Yes. It comes out on its own."

Daimon looked at me in disbelief. “Wow. That’s—cool.”

“Totally!” Kabe said.

“You surprise me, Daimon. Your girlfriend nearly died because of my blip.”

“Eh, she’s fine.”

I liked Daimon.

“You understand I won’t play you much at the beginning?” he said.

“Yes, I would prefer that.”

“Great! So do you want to be on the team?”

I paused, looking from Daimon to Kabe. “Sure!”

Daimon punched the air in triumph. “You’ve made my day, Loddy.”

“All right!” Kabe said, hugging me.

“Just keep me updated on your lessons, okay?” Daimon winked.

“I can do that.”

“We’re playing Mackrivoy on Friday. They’ll be a hard team to beat, but you’ll just observe.”

“Okay! Can do!”

“It’s time to huddle!”

On cue, everyone ran—or in Melee and Blaze’s case, walked—to the sidelines.

Daimon addressed the group. “I have great news: Loddy is on the team!”

Resno smiled, Meena yelled *yay,* and Melee and Blaze rolled their eyes.

“This is going to be a good year! I’m content with where we are, but we’ve got a lot of work to do! All hands in! Duel it on three! One, two, three—"

"*Duel it*!"

"I'll see everyone Friday! Let's beat Mackrivoy!"

Meena caught up with me as we left the grobe. "I'm so excited you're on the team!"

"Me, too!"

"Did you have trouble with the formations?"

"Of course not," Kabe said. "Her teacher was the best."

"Whatever you say."

Walking into the lobby, I spotted Taurik. When he saw Kabe, his eyes glossed over.

"Hey, Taurik," Meena said, batting her eyelashes. My feelings of warmth towards her were replaced by deep annoyance.

"Hey, Taurik." Kabe's tone was uneasy.

"Hello, Meena." Taurik was clearly ignoring Kabe. He turned to me. "Are you ready?"

"Yes. I'll see you guys later." I smiled.

"Bye, Loddy!" Meena's smile never disappeared.

"Bye." Kabe's voice lacked life. His eyes were filled with longing.

Leaving the grobe, I wondered why Taurik and Kabe were so cold toward each other. The reason was probably another secret Taurik wouldn't tell me.

10

MIND CONTROL

"Taurik, why did you ignore Kabe?"

He didn't answer.

"Taurik?"

"I'm just—not crazy about the guy, okay?"

"Why not?"

Taurik dodged eye contact. "He—he makes me uneasy."

"I see." My heart fluttered at the possibility that he was jealous.

"He isn't a good guy, Loddy." Fear was in his eyes.

"He *seems* pleasant. A bit touchy—"

"*Touchy*?" He spoke through clenched teeth. "He *touched* you?"

"He showed me some fight formations—"

Taurik enunciated each word: "*Don't-ever-let-him-touch-you-again.*"

"Why? What has he done?"

"I can't say. It's—a stupid secret." He grabbed my arms and looked into my eyes. "Don't ever be alone with him. *Promise me.*"

His intensity was convincing. "I—I promise."

When we arrived at Chaste Palez, Taurik said, "When do you want to finish the questionnaire?"

"How about tomorrow after my lessons with Kallisto?"

"Sure." As he turned to leave, I could see the rage still in his eyes.

"Taurik?"

He stopped.

"Don't hurt Kabe. Promise me."

He hesitated. In a voice choked with agony, he said, "Promise."

In my room, I saw that my heart anthilomy had changed. Taurik had tried to shove Zander out.

Within a few months, Zander could be absent from my anthilomy completely.

I spotted Cannon walking through the Chaste Palez lobby the next day. When she saw me, she ran to catch up.

"Hey!" she said, smiling.

"Hey."

"I have a question for you."

"A question?" I hated her questions as they almost always involved something personal. "Yeah! Besides the duel, do you have plans on Friday night? By the way, congrats on making the team!"

"Thanks. Um, no plans."

"Then you can come to my sleepover!"

I regretted my honesty. "Where?"

"In my room, duh! So you'll be there?"

"I'm, uh, I don't know." I didn't want to be stuck in

a room with Melee and Blaze.

As if she read my mind, Cannon said, "Don't worry. Melee and Blaze won't be there."

"Oh, well, I—"

"*Please! Please! Please*!"

I didn't know how I could say no at that point. "Okay."

Clapping her hands, she said, "Yay! We'll have *so* much fun!"

"I'm sure."

"Well, I have homework to finish before class. See you later!"

During quintessence, Cannon sat next to me and chattered non-stop. I was thankful Professor Biv didn't chastise us for all the noise Cannon was making. I would have much preferred that she be like Evily and have nothing to do with me.

Calix was incredulous when I told him about Cannon's invitation. "A sleepover? Is she for real?"

"She seems intent on becoming friends."

"What does she want?"

"Taurik?" We giggled. "No, I don't know what she wants."

"There's no harm indulging her for a while. Maybe you can figure her out."

"Maybe"

"Who knows?" He smiled sarcastically. "Maybe you'll end up liking her."

I rolled my eyes. "I don't know about that."

Raising his hands in mock surrender, he said,

"Anything is possible."

Before History of Aspasia, I told Carrigan about Cannon.

"And that is my problem how?"

"I thought you might have some advice for me."

"Umm, no."

I sighed. "Thanks anyway, Carrigan."

"Hello, everyone." Yttira's baritone filled the room. "I have a most interesting lesson prepared for today."

I perked up.

"Today, we're discussing the Aspasian War catalyst who happened to be—a baby."

Most people looked confused while others, like Carrigan, lit up.

"Could you explain, Carrigan?"

"Yes, sir. The baby was Deo's daughter."

"Her name?"

"Lodesyia."

My heart beat faster. Meda had addressed me by that name in her letter.

The classroom setting took on the appearance of a spacious room. No one was in the room save for a baby in an exquisite pearl crib that seemed to rock itself. When Yttira zoomed in on the crib, we saw that the pale baby was a beautiful girl with platinum locks and the most innocent air about her.

"She's beautiful, isn't she?"

Everyone, even Carrigan, nodded.

"*This* is Lodesyia Clevist, the Princess of Aspasia."

Lodesyia Clevist? With a quavering voice, I asked,

"How did she start the war?"

"The scene will reveal all."

As soon as the scene unfroze, a silhouette jumped into the room. The unrecognizable figure was thin and nimble. He—or she—was a walking shadow that looked down at the baby, grabbed her and then leaped out the window.

"Lodesyia was kidnapped 180 years ago. We still don't know who did it. Because of lack of information, the kidnapper in my scene is a black silhouette. However, the academic community is ninety percent sure that someone from Alexander's entourage is responsible."

I wondered why Kesta had never told me the name of Deo's child.

"Alexander and Deo loved to play pranks on one another. It was their way of relieving stress. Being gods, they had unlimited resources to draw on for their antics. Thus, their pranks are monumental compared with anything we normal citizens could implement. For instance, they could make an entire building disappear for fun. While this kind of prank may sound intriguing, it ultimately led to the princess's kidnapping.

"You see, the stakes became so high with these outlandish pranks that in Alexander and Deo's minds, breaking the law was the only way to win. So it is widely believed that Alexander had the princess kidnapped to ensure his success.

"The next part of the story is controversial. When Alexander was accused of kidnapping the princess, he denied it, so Deo sent spies to Alexander's quasian to find her. Alexander found out and became enraged, and his denial continued.

"After realizing that Alexander wasn't budging, Deo kidnapped Alexander's youngest son, a prince. Alexander was livid. He had the princess all along, so in his fury, he accidentally strangled her. Deo didn't see the death as an accident, so he killed the prince and declared war on Alexander.

"Some say Alexander strangled Princess Lodesyia on purpose, while others maintain that Deo purposely misplaced her so he could declare war on Alexander. Matters weren't helped when another of Alexander's sons disappeared a few years ago. No one knows where he went, but I'm sure that opened fresh wounds for Alexander.

"Whatever you believe, the war is still raging, and it doesn't show any signs of abating."

"Don't some people believe the princess is still alive?" Carrigan asked.

"Ah, yes." Yttira chuckled. "Radicals believe someone kidnapped the princess while she was in Alexander's possession, and that the kidnapper replaced her with a doppelganger before Alexander strangled her. I highly doubt this theory."

"Why?" I asked.

"Because the radicals believe that whoever kidnapped the princess from Alexander plans to use her to overthrow the gods. The idea is too outlandish."

I believed the idea was possible.

After History of Aspasia, I decided to attempt prying my appenda-port from Professor Zazz's hands again. But for the first time since completing my appenda-port, I couldn't find it in Professor Zazz's classroom. I asked him where it was.

"The headmiztrezz wanted it."

Oh no. "Why?"

The Professor's eyes dropped. "Iz . . . nothing."

"But it's *my* appenda-port." I didn't yell, which I thought showed major self-control. Every second without my appenda-port prolonged my discovering whether Aunt Maggie and Uncle William were still alive. Once I had it, Taurik and I could transport ourselves back to Sun City to see if Uncle William and Aunt Maggie were still there.

Professor Zazz's pupil-less eyes veered upward, and I saw shame in them. *Had Kallisto confiscated my appenda-port?*

"I have zomewhere to be." He rushed out of the room.

Are you kidding? I feared that Kallisto had taken my appenda-port for other reasons than to rob Professor Zazz of research.

Walking into aphotology, I couldn't find Taurik. That didn't surprise me since he was ever-faithful to his reputation for chronic lateness. Sitting down, a high breathy voice whispered, "Pssst. Hey." The intonation reminded me of a little girl's. I looked around, but everyone in the room was a teenager.

"It's me, Malicious." She was whisper-chasing, sending a spoken message only I could hear. She waved, then cupped her mouth and hissed, "I wanted to introduce myself."

"Nice to meet you," I mouthed.

"If you need anything from me or any of Taurik's friends, let me know. We'll be happy to help." She gave me a thumbs-up before turning around.

Taurik walked into the classroom with Professor Nazzir. I wondered if Taurik had told his friends to reach out.

He sat beside me. "What's up?"

"Cannon and Malicious are acting uncharacteristically warm toward me. Did you say something to Malicious?"

"I told my friends to be friendly to you. Is that okay?"

"I guess." I smiled.

"What about Cannon? Is she acting weirder than usual?"

"She invited me to a sleepover this Friday, and I said I would go."

"Really?" In a high-pitched girly voice he asked, "Are you painting each other's nails and talking about boys?"

I thumped his arm.

"Ow! I was just kidding."

"Mm-hmm."

"So what do girls do at sleepovers?"

"I don't know. I'm regretting saying yes now."

"Cancel. You can do something with me."

He made it sound so easy, but I couldn't cancel on her. What if the sleepover was an olive branch?

"I can't."

"Why not? She treats us like dirt. No reason we can't treat her the same way."

"You *do* treat her like dirt, Taurik."

He shrugged.

"I wonder if she has an ulterior motive."

"Of course she does."

"What if she's misunderstood? You of all people should sympathize."

"Nah. She's just wrapped around the headmistress's little finger."

I noticed Pilmus then, his neck craned toward us as far as it could reach. I lowered my voice. "Remember, we're in mixed company."

"I don't care. Cannon knows I think she's scum."

I wanted to tell Taurik about the discussion with Professor Zazz, but Pilmus was still listening.

"How are we doing with our projects?" Professor Nazzir asked.

No group volunteered its progress.

"Very well. Mr. Night, how is your project going?"

"We aren't done, but we're hoping to present our project tomorrow. We don't want to give anything away."

I rolled my eyes.

"What a shame. Could you at least give us a sneak peek?"

"Professor, the excitement this class will experience at our presentation will be nothing less than—unquantifiable."

Ugh.

"I'm sure, Mr. Night. We're all looking forward to it. Next!"

Out of class and out of Pilmus's earshot, Taurik said, "Did you get the appenda-port?"

"No."

He was indignant. "Then I'm getting it myself. Is Zazz still in his classroom?"

I grabbed him. "*He* doesn't have it anymore."

Taurik stopped. "Where is it?"

"*She* has it."

Pure rage flashed in his eyes. "*She* has it?"

I nodded.

He shook free and started in the direction of Kallisto's office, muttering under his breath.

I caught up with him and grabbed his arm again. "Taurik, I wouldn't do that!"

"Loddy," he said through clenched teeth. "This isn't *any of her business*."

"We can't anger her anymore."

He broke free from my grasp. An extra reserve of energy awakened within me, and I clenched Taurik's arm with new strength.

He stared at me in disbelief. "Let go, Loddy!"

I maneuvered him into an empty classroom with strength I didn't know I had. Blocking the doorway, I let his arm go. "Be quiet," I whispered. "I don't want Pilmus to hear what I'm about to tell you."

His eyes still registered amazement that I had forcibly guided him to another room.

"I'm afraid she took the appenda-port because she

suspects something."

"Of course she does. I'm tired of her manipulating everyone to get what she wants." He was a few inches from my face.

"Taurik, don't say anything to her about this."

His eyes were intense. "Give me one reason I shouldn't."

Hypnotized by Taurik's alluring eyes, I lost all sense of my surroundings. I knew he wasn't using his ability to take advantage of me. For the first time, I let my defenses down. We leaned in until our lips met.

As his lips pressed into mine, his peace at having finally reached this point in our relationship flowed into me. His genuine happiness radiated my own.

Leaning away from one another, we continued staring into each other's eyes. Taurik's were filled with a contentment I had never seen.

"Reason enough for me."

I'd finally won. "Remember, one of us still has to see her."

"Oh, yeah. You're confined to a room with the dragon lady for hours."

"Don't remind me. I need to go. I can't be late."

"Because of me?"

"Yes, because of you. So if you will excuse me—" I turned to leave, but his outstretched arm stopped me.

His eyes were warm. "I like this."

"I do, too." To finally say it felt liberating.

"See you after your lessons?"

"Yes."

"May I pick our workspace?"

I was surprised that he wanted to choose. "Sure."

"I wouldn't care otherwise, but Malicious wants to properly meet you."

"Oh?"

"Yeah. In fact, I'd like to introduce you to all my friends."

Besides frightening me, his friends seemed, well, different. With forced politeness, I asked, "Really?"

Seeing through my façade, he shook his head. "Loddy, they'll like you. I promise." "If you say so."

"If they don't, they'll answer to me."

I laughed, but I was still skeptical. "Where are we meeting?"

"Dreg's?"

Wow. I never thought I would ever step into an aphotic hangout. "Is it safe?"

He grinned. "Yes. Why wouldn't it be?"

"Because a lot of aphotics go there."

He laughed. "Loddy, aphotics aren't bad people. We're just misunderstood. You should know that after having classes with us."

"I guess so."

"Loddy, trust me."

Looking into his eyes, I knew everything would work out. I smiled and nodded. "Okay."

"See you after your lessons."

When I arrived at the power practice gym, I saw a canceller I didn't know with Kallisto who, along with a black cloak, wore an irritated look.

"You're late."

I was amazed at how quickly she could diminish a good mood. "I apologize."

"Come here." She slipped her cloak off showcasing a skin-tight black outfit that covered her entire body, accentuating all her curves.

I walked toward her, smiling at the canceller.

"He's here to monitor."

I nodded.

"I'm going to teach you how to control your mind under any circumstances. So clear your head. You have five minutes."

I closed my eyes, but clearing my head was difficult. After four minutes, I had cleared it of everything except the most pressing matters: Aunt Maggie, Uncle William, and Professor Omega.

Five minutes passed. "Time's up," she said. "Well?"

"I got close." I was sheepish, but I knew that wouldn't get me anywhere with her.

"Fine. Five more minutes then. Try harder this time."

I closed my eyes and again cleared my mind of everything except for my most important thoughts. I couldn't stop worrying because I had no control over them. I tried focusing on a sound in the room to drown out the thoughts, but the room was silent.

"Well?" Her expression was cold. She wasn't making it any easier for me to relax.

"I can't clear out everything."

"What exactly can't you clear out?"

"Cannon wants to have a sleepover," I lied. "But I don't know what to talk about with her."

Irritated, she breathed in heavily. "What else?"

"I'm nervous about being on the duel team."

"What else?"

"I'm still trying to fit in here."

"Is that it?"

"I think so."

"Loddy, if you can't clear trivial thoughts, you can't handle opposing the most powerful beings in Aspasia."

"I know."

She sighed. "We can't move on until you clear your head. A clear head is a sign of complete mind control, and that is the goal. Try again."

I tried repeatedly for the next hour, but I was unsuccessful. Once, I got close to clearing out my worry over Professor Omega, but then the thought slithered back in. Aunt Maggie and Uncle William were always present.

Kallisto was aloof toward me the entire time. She was probably getting back at me for my not having spoken up when Taurik went after her.

"Well?"

I shook my head in defeat.

She sighed. "I don't understand. You've been trying for an hour."

"It's difficult."

"I know, but you should have at least made *some* progress by now."

"You aren't making it any easier."

She grabbed my shoulders and forced me to stare her straight in the eye. "You will *not* speak to me the way he does."

I shrugged her hands away and continued staring fearlessly at her. My face was as detached as hers had been during the entire training session.

"I can't believe you're allowing him to influence you. I thought you were on my side." "I've promised to help overthrow Deo. That doesn't mean you can dictate with whom I interact."

"*But I'm your mother*!"

I winced. The way she tried twisting my emotions was sick, but I had to play along. "Our relationship doesn't change anything."

She grimaced, and her face looked ten years older. Flames spurted in her eyes. "If that's the way you want it . . ."

I stood my ground. "No harm comes to Taurik."

Eyebrows raised, she said, "I would never hurt Mr. Night." But dark humor was in her tone.

"To ensure your promise, I offer an ultimatum: If Taurik is harmed, I won't help you."

A hint of surprise was in her eyes. "Wow. In no time, he has imprinted your personality. What happened to the meek, innocent girl Kesta brought to me?"

"Do I have your word that no harm will come to him?"

She hesitated, her eyes narrowed. "You have my word. Now clear your mind."

Her tone was more understanding for the rest of the

session. Twenty minutes later, her voice hopeful, she asked, "Well?"

"No."

She exhaled, but not menacingly. "We're done for today."

I sighed in relief.

"We'll meet again in two days, so I encourage you to practice."

"Yes, ma'am."

"You may go."

I started toward the exit when I remembered that I had a question for her. "You have my appenda-port?"

The coldness returned to her voice. "I do."

"May I have it?"

"Not until you can control your mind."

So that's how it's going to be.

"You may go."

11

ACCESS

At Dreg's Eatery, I told Taurik that Kallisto would not give me my appenda-port.

"Are you serious?"

"Yes."

"Ugh! She has her hand in everything at this school."

"Well, she *is* the headmistress. I wonder if she suspects that you and I are trying to leave Aspasia."

"Why would she?"

Remembering the warning in Meda's note about people not being what they seemed, I looked around to see if anyone was listening. "Something tells me she has spies."

"Calix and Carrigan?"

"No! Cannon."

"But she's an idiot."

"She did snitch to the headmistress about your being in Chaste Palez."

"Yeah, but that doesn't mean she's a spy."

"I wonder if she's having this sleepover to interrogate me for Kallisto."

"I don't know. But here come my friends, so take a

break from being detective and be sociable."

"Hey, guys!" Malicious called, waving. She was wearing a holey magenta shirt which revealed a sparkly, silver undershirt. What drew the most attention was her glittery pink tutu. Instead of ballet slippers, she pirouetted in pink flats.

Cash's hair was spiked and colored the chartreuse of newly cut grass. Cassius's short, scarlet hair was styled to the side. He had that depressed expression I now associated with him.

Bite, who proudly sported a gash on his left arm, wore a dumb smile, and Draegan, who was clad in black, had a despondent expression that was even more pronounced than Cassius'.

"Hey, guys! I'd like to introduce Loddy."

Malicious, Cash, and Bite smiled while Cassius nodded and Draegan shifted his gaze slightly. "It's *so* nice to finally meet you without having to use secret messages," Malicious said, sitting next to me. "How do you like aphotology?"

"It's, um, different."

"You probably think all aphotics are evil, don't you?" She winked at Taurik.

"He told you what I said?"

She had the kind of surprised look one would get from an actor onstage. "No. What are you talking about?"

I giggled. "Okay. So I was a little prejudiced."

"Or a lot," said Cash. His voice was higher than I expected.

"Taurik, your friends are so subtle."

Cash shrugged his shoulders. “I call ‘em like I see ‘em.”

“You’ve never been prejudiced?”

Placing his hand beneath his chin and staring off into space, he pretended to be pondering the question. “Nope!”

I giggled. “Kuddos to you for being inhuman.”

“I take pride in my inhuman-ness.” He smiled, showcasing all his teeth.

When neither Cassius nor Draegan spoke, Malicious took the initiative. “Cassius and Draegan don’t talk much. They’re our thinkers, right guys?”

They nodded slightly.

“They’ll open up more once they get to know you.”

I smiled at Cassius and Draegan. With their unapproachable exteriors, it was hard for me to believe that they could open up to anyone.

Taurik turned to me. “Now you know everyone. Ready to eat?”

“Yes, I’m starving.”

“Food! Food! Food!” Bite yelled.

On Malicious’ recommendation, I ordered the smoked jeex along with a Personal Nightmare, a drink that she said was sweet apart from its unique flavor.

While we waited for our drinks, Taurik brought his friends up to speed. “Loddy thinks Cannon’s a spy for the headmistress.”

“It wouldn’t surprise me,” Cash said.

I made eye contact with Taurik. “We can talk about this later.”

“Why? They can be trusted.”

“Yep. We’ve been screened, Princess,” Cash said. His eyes were the same chartreuse as his hair.

“So why do you believe she’s a spy?” Malicious asked.

“She’s just been acting oddly, and she seems chummier than usual with the headmistress.”

“I think she’s too stupid to be a spy,” Taurik said.

Cash nodded. “I side with Taurik. I don’t think I’ve ever seen her around the administration building. Carrigan’s there all the time, though.”

“He is?” I couldn’t imagine why.

“Yeah, I’ve seen him there a half dozen times since school started.”

“Really!”

“Yeah, I can’t imagine why he’d have to be there that often.”

“I can’t, either. I’ll ask him.”

The waiter brought our drinks. My Personal Nightmare was black and slushy and served in a large glass bowl with a thin handle. What made the drink like no other was that it was swirling like a tornado.

I turned to Malicious. “It moves?”

“Yes! I didn’t want to ruin the surprise! Isn’t it cool?”

It *was* cool. I had never had a drink that actually moved by itself.

“Aren’t you going to try it?”

“Of course.” I took a sip. My tongue felt on fire but without heat, followed by a slightly sweet aftertaste.

"Do you like it?" Malicious asked, surveying my reaction.

"Yes, it's—unusual."

She smiled. "I'm *so* glad you like it!"

"So you're friends with Calix and Carrigan?" Cash asked me.

"I am."

"Okay." He nodded, making an effort to keep his mouth shut.

I looked at Taurik. "Don't you trust them?"

"Eh, they just aren't our type," he said.

I couldn't understand why Cash and Taurik had reservations about Calix and Carrigan. They were some of the best people I had met since arriving at Abervania.

When the waiter brought our food, my meat resembled steak swimming in a scarlet gravy. Taking a bite, I registered the muskiness which characterizes any type of smoked meat before tasting a mix of tang and sweetness.

"Well?" Malicious asked.

"It's delicious." I stared at Bite who, animal-like, was devouring a piece of black meat.

Taurik noticed me gawking at him. "Bite loves his food almost as much as he loves fighting."

"Fighting?"

"Yeah. How do you think he got that gash on his arm?"

After dinner, Taurik and I thanked his friends for joining us. Malicious, Cash, and Bite were enthusiastic with their good-byes, while Cash told me he hoped I realized that aphotics weren't evil now, and Draegan and Cassius just gaped at me.

After leaving Dreg's, I realized Taurik and I still hadn't finished our project. "What about the questionnaire?"

He feigned mock concern. "Oh, no. Whatever will we do?"

"Why aren't you worried?"

"Because I already answered all the questions except one." He smiled smugly.

"Which one?"

He stared me straight in the eye. "Do you feel like you know your partner better now?"

"I do." Even though I still didn't know as much as I wanted, I'd learned a lot about Taurik. "And you?"

"Most definitely." He closed in for a kiss.

When our lips met, I again tingled from the pleasant pressure. This time, he took me in his arms and pressed me against his solid chest, and I felt protected.

Leaning back, he asked, "Do you think we're ready to present tomorrow?"

"Probably not as well as Professor Nazzir expects."

"How about we wing it and hope for the best?"

"Fine with me. I'm so ready for bed."

"Me, too."

After Taurik left me at the Chaste Palez steps, I acknowledged how easy kissing him was, even with Zander at the back of my mind. For the first time, I realized that I loved Taurik Night, and he loved me. I would sleep better than I had in months.

The next day I sat with Taurik and his friends during consummation. People kept staring at our table in surprise, but I didn't care.

I motioned Calix and Carrigan over, though Calix's body tensed and Carrigan's eyes became slits. As they trudged toward our table, I leaned over to Taurik and whispered, "Be nice."

"Hey, Loddy." Calix's tone was friendly, but he didn't sit down like I expected. Carrigan said nothing.

"Hey, guys!" Taurik said. "Won't you take a seat?"

"Of course," Calix said.

I introduced Calix and Carrigan to the rest of Taurik's friends. Draegan and Cassius avoided eye contact, but Malicious and Cash beamed.

While Taurik and his friends were chatting among themselves, I turned to Calix. "Are you coming to my game tomorrow? It'll be my first duel."

"I'll be there!" Calix sounded enthusiastic and glanced at Carrigan.

"Maybe," Carrigan said.

"Well, at least one of us will be there. Who's your opponent?"

"Mackrivoy, but I won't be dueling. I'll just be watching from the bench."

"That's okay. You're still a part of the team," Calix said. "How was practice?"

"It went well. Did you know Meena's on the team?"

"She is? No, I didn't know that. But I haven't gone to many duels," he added.

"She's another friendly face. So, Carrigan," I continued, "I have a question."

He reluctantly looked at me. "Y—yes?"

"I hear you spend a lot of time in the administration building. Do you have a secret project?"

"No." But his eyes lit up, and he straightened in his seat.

"Are you sure?"

"Who told you I spend a lot of time there?"

Cash zeroed in on our conversation, and Taurik and Malicious stopped talking.

"Someone in one of my classes," I shrugged.

"Oh. Well, I don't have anything going on."

"Okay, I was just curious." I made eye contact with Cash who smiled.

That afternoon, when I arrived for power practice, the atmosphere in the gym felt different. I identified the source of the shift as the last person I'd seen there the day before. Except now, she wore a black pantsuit and stood next to Professor Pex.

Kallisto smiled. "Hello, everyone. I'm going to observe your class today as it has been a while since I've done so. I don't want my presence to affect your performance, so pretend I'm not here. Can you do that?"

We nodded.

"Wonderful. As you were." Kallisto walked to the far sideline and climbed up to the reviewer's seat.

Once she was out of earshot, everyone sighed in relief.

"We're fighting today!" Professor Pex yelled. "Get

with your team and confer for five minutes!"

Wonderful, I thought. Last time we fought, Cassie and her team had handily beaten my team. However, since I had learned some new fight formations, I hoped this match might have a different outcome.

I strolled over to my group, which consisted of Calix, Evily, and Meena. Evily still avoided communication with us, so we essentially had a three-person team. Since Valisa had left the other team, they only had three people as well: Blaze, Cannon, and Sulwen.

Cannon raised her hand and yelled, "Professor Pex! The teams aren't even anymore!"

"They're not always going to be even, Cannon!" he called, making his ascent to the game pedestal from where he could observe the room. From there, he would create the illusion that made it seem as if we could hurt one another.

"What's our strategy?" Meena asked me.

"What can Sulwen do?" I asked.

"He's a light manipulator."

"So he'll be able to create illusions like Melee does," Calix added.

"No, he won't," Evily said.

We were reluctant to reply for fear of saying the wrong thing. I decided to take a chance. "What makes you say that?"

She made eye contact with me before looking down. "Because he's very messy." Her high-pitched voice was musical, soft but not breathy. "He doesn't have the control to manipulate light to that degree. If anything, he'll shoot light rays at us, though not with any accuracy."

We continued staring at her trying to process that she was speaking to us for the first time. I was overjoyed. "So we shouldn't worry about him?"

"I didn't say that. He'll be messy, but he'll still be a problem unless someone takes him out soon. That person has to be fast in case he or she has to dodge light rays."

"I'm fast!" Meena said.

"Okay. You handle Sulwen." Evily said. "Now for Cannon."

"She'll rely on hand-to-hand combat since her ability to read memories isn't practical for offense," Calix said.

"That's true. Do you think you could overpower her?"

"I'll try!"

"What about Blaze?" I asked. Overpowering her would be hardest.

"Well, since Blaze relies on flying to get near her opponents, we should attach her to something stationary."

"Like what?"

"The floor?"

"How can we—?"

"*I'll* make sure it happens," Evily interrupted. "Then, Loddy, all you have to do is take her out. You can do that, right?"

I didn't want our team depending on me to deliver the final punch to Blaze. "Well—" "Time!" Professor Pex yelled.

Immediately we were plunged into the illusion. Our surroundings had not changed, but I knew we were no longer in reality. I scanned the area and saw Melee running toward Sulwen who was attempting to pound her with concentrated light blasts. Thankfully, she dodged every one of them. Nearby, Calix and Cannon were engaged in hand-to-hand combat, and both were holding up well.

Looking up, I searched for Blaze in midair, but she was nowhere to be seen.

"Loddy!" Evily yelled.

Expecting to see Blaze beating Evily, I looked in the direction of her voice, only to be taken by surprise. Hunched over, hands outstretched, Evily had somehow made the ground mesh with Blaze's feet, confining her to one spot. Using all her strength, Blaze was struggling to break free.

"I can't hold her long!" Evily yelled. "Hit her now!"

Oh no, not me. I sprinted over to Blaze who glared at me.

"Go on!" Evily shouted.

I hesitated, trying to think, before inching closer to the thrashing Blaze.

"Attack from a distance!" Evily yelled. "She might hit you if you get too close."

I didn't know how to attack from a distance. I closed my eyes and tried to concentrate. I tried clearing my brain, but, of course, I was only able to clear the minor thoughts plaguing me. With pain in her voice, Evily yelped, "When you're ready!"

I cleared more, but it still wasn't enough. Evily groaned as the pain overwhelmed her. I closed my eyes again and forced myself to clear my brain of every thought.

Then, everything was gone.

With this clarity came a consciousness of which I had never been aware: another being was inside me—the dark phoenix—and it wanted out. But something on the outside seemed to hinder the dark phoenix.

I opened my eyes. Instantly I felt empowered by energy from deep inside—energy that was mine to command. Expecting that energy to come forth, I reached out—but nothing happened.

Hunching more every second, Evily screamed, "What's wrong?"

"I don't know. I feel like something should be happening."

Then Blaze broke out of Evily's trap and went for her. She punched her, and Evily flew backwards.

"No!" I watched Evily fly the length of the gym before slamming into the far wall, leaving a crater-sized dent.

Then fear flooded every crevice of my body as Blaze came for me. I caught her glare before she punched me. Fiery pain exploded as every bone in my face broke. I blacked out, thanking the heavens that the attack was fake.

When I awoke, I was standing exactly where I had been before the illusion took over. I looked at my team with remorse. "Sorry, guys."

"It's okay," Meena said. "At least we got closer this time."

I could always count on Meena to encourage me, but Evily huffed in irritation.

"Wow, you guys have really improved!" Professor

Biv was beaming. “You had me believing you were going to win.”

“Evily helped us all, sir. She was great. I just wasn’t on.”

“Really? Is this true, Evily?”

She looked at him, and I thought she wasn’t going to reply. “I just gave my teammates pointers, sir. Excuse me.” She walked to the locker rooms.

The headmistress joined us, and Professor Pex tensed up. “Wasn’t that great, headmistress?”

“It was—” her eyes settled on me “—interesting.”

“Yes, well, I’m proud of them!” The professor smiled at me nervously.

“I must be going,” Kallisto said. “Loddy, a word?”

As I followed her into the hallway outside the gym, Professor Pex called, “Goodbye, Headmistress.” I could hear the elation in his voice over having escaped the monster’s presence.

Kallisto glared at me. “What happened?”

“I don’t know.”

“Did you clear your head?”

“Yes, I actually did.”

Surprise rose in her eyes, but she was quick to squelch it. “I don’t understand.”

“I cleared my head, and I sensed the phoenix.”

“But?”

“But the phoenix felt hindered by something around me, so it couldn’t come out.”

Her brow furrowed. “*It* felt hindered, or *you* felt hindered?”

"I guess we both felt hindered."

"I see. So it felt hindered by something?"

"Yes."

"How many chastes are in the class besides you?"

I counted. "Four." I realized then the majority of the class was comprised of chastes.

"I see." She paused. "You may go back to class."

I turned and started for the gym.

"Oh, and Loddy?"

"Yes?"

"It would be best if you don't access the phoenix unless I'm present. Understood?"

"Yes, ma'am."

12

DUEL

During aphotology, Taurik and I presented our questionnaire findings. I couldn't believe we had finished.

"Through this project," Taurik began, "I've learned that people are multifaceted. Instead of being comprised of good and evil facets, we have a mix. That we assign a stereotype to every person is unfair. I know we stereotype to simplify, but we're much more complicated and beautiful. I see that now, and I hope you will, too, if you haven't already."

When my turn came, I knew my conclusions wouldn't top Taurik's. "I learned that one doesn't have to know everything about a person. Sometimes, trusting the other and knowing that he or she has your best interests at heart is the only option. Of course, not everyone can be trusted, but that's what makes this faith all the more special. With those who live up to that trust, long-term advantages await."

I thought we had summed up each other well. Professor Nazzir did, too, as he gave us high marks.

Exiting the classroom, I turned to Taurik. "What you said about me was really sweet."

"Eh, I can be nice." He winked. "Just don't get used to it."

I smiled. Walking down the hallway, I realized that, for once, I didn't have plans after school. Secretly, I hoped Taurik would ask me out on a date, but I didn't know how to broach the subject without seeming overeager.

"I'm meeting the guys tonight. We've been wanting to go out for a while."

So much for a date. "Right. I'm sure you'll have a great time."

"We should do something tomorrow night."

"I can't. I have plans with Cannon, remember?" I would have saved the date had I not remembered the sleepover.

"Oh, yeah. I forgot about your gig with the bloodsucker. I can't wait to hear how it goes."

"Yeah. . ."

He grinned. "Hey, look at the bright side. You can finally probe the enemy."

The next day, Friday, I went to another training session with Kallisto since I wasn't dueling. Walking into the power practice gym, I saw Kallisto with the canceller. Her expression was neutral but not as cold as it had been during the previous session.

"Start clearing your mind," she told me. "If you're able to clear it like you did in power practice, we'll start with Beginners' Tactics."

"What if the phoenix comes out?"

"The canceller will take care of the phoenix. When it comes out, you need to use every thought you have to smother it."

"How do I do that?"

"I can't explain. You'll know when it comes out. Just concentrate."

I sat down, but when I tried to clear my mind, needles of pain struck every crevice of my cerebrum.

The dark phoenix's voice took me by surprise. *Well, well, well. Isn't this unexpected? You finally summoned me. I must say it took you long enough.*

The phoenix' breathy voice chilled my entire body. I began to drift in and out of consciousness as it tried to overtake me. Kallisto was staring at me curiously.

"I'm here!" I yelled without warning in a deranged voice.

Realization hit Kallisto. "Loddy, concentrate every element of your being on the phoenix. Smother it with your thoughts. Do you understand?"

"I can't fo—" I was unable to concentrate on speech. Kallisto became an indistinct silhouette as I tried summoning every thought to quell the dark phoenix. I seized a few thoughts, but I couldn't capture enough. The phoenix snapped the last strand of my consciousness, and I blacked out.

I woke up, and, little by little, my surroundings lost their hazy quality. Kallisto was still the same distance away as she had been when I started concentrating. *Thank goodness for the canceller.*

"Well?"

"Smothering the phoenix was hard."

"Of course it was. Did you think it would be easy?"

"The phoenix talked to me."

"It did?" Suspense filled her eyes. "What did it say?"

"It provoked me over how long I took to summon it."

"You must never communicate with the phoenix."

"Why?"

"Because communicating makes it easier for the phoenix to take hold of your mind."

I wondered if that was the real reason. "Okay."

"Good. Now clear your thoughts."

I closed my eyes and ignored my surroundings.

You know what's funny? Neither of us likes her. We should team up and beat her. You don't even know the truth behind what she did to you years ago.

Without thinking, I asked, "What did she do?"

"Now!" Kallisto shouted.

The dark phoenix's voice went mute. I was amazed at how speedily the canceller drove the phoenix out of my mind.

Kallisto looked worried. She took me by the shoulders and stared into my eyes. "I don't want you clearing your head unless Kesta or I are with you. Do you understand?" Her voice was stern.

"Yes." Had the phoenix wanted to tell me a secret Kallisto didn't want me to hear?

"I'm serious, Loddy. I suspect you won't obey me when it comes to Taurik, but I'm begging you: Do *not* clear your head by yourself. Clearing your head could be detrimental not only to you but to the campus."

Whoa. What didn't she want me to know? "Why are you just now telling me this? Before, clearing my head was acceptable no matter what the circumstances."

"Because I didn't think you'd master clearing your head so soon."

"I see." I decided not to press the point. "May I go now? I need to change before the duel."

Without making eye contact, she said, "Yes, you may go."

I was furious that Kallisto fed me crucial information as she saw fit. The more I thought about it, I wondered if she even contemplated the potential consequences of her actions. When I walked into the Grobe, both teams were already present. I couldn't find Melee and Blaze, though.

Mackrivoy had five players. Their captain was a dark-skinned, muscular African-American and had the same build as Daimon.

Only one girl was on Mackrivoy's team, and she, too, was African-American. She was slender and toned and had a more intimidating gaze than the captain.

The remaining three players didn't resemble each other in the least. A large, heavy-built, African-American fellow looked like he could have picked up half of our team and catapulted us back up the field. The pale guy with dingy blond hair didn't look athletically fit, so I assumed that his abilities must have compensated for his appearance.

The medium-built Asian was the most beautiful person on the team—including the girl. His stunning eyes reminded me of the ocean on a sunny day. In fact, they were so distinctive that they dazzled from the other side of the field.

Kabe and Meena spotted me approaching and waved. When I finally made it to our side of the field, Daimon said, "Hey, Loddy! Ready to watch your first duel?"

"I guess so. I'm still nervous for you guys, though."

"Don't worry about us. We're old pros. Right, Kabe?"

"Yeah!"

What Taurik had told me about Kabe was hard to believe. He seemed so genuine.

Stealing a glance at Mackrivoy, Daimon asked, "What do you think of the competition?"

"They look intimidating."

"Eh." He smiled with a twinkle in his eye.

Pointing to the first guy I'd seen, I asked, "Is *he* the captain?"

"Yes. Tervik Lavister. Probably our biggest threat, but not one we can't handle." He winked and jogged off to tend to Resno who was reviewing last-minute combat moves.

Kabe slid beside me. "Hey! You excited?"

"I am. I just don't want anyone to get hurt."

"Eh, that's part of it. Say, is Taurik okay?"

"Yeah."

"He doesn't want me around you, does he?"

"He's just protective of me."

Kabe nodded. "I understand. He's never liked me. I don't know why."

"I don't either."

Melee and Blaze showed up then, and Cannon walked in with her fellow cheerleaders the metaprites, who appeared to be gossiping. Seeing me, she smiled and waved.

I watched my team file into the dressing room, then started to follow behind them. Kabe grabbed my shoulder.

"I hope this doesn't mean we can't be friends." Pure genuineness sparkled in his eyes.

"Of course not."

He smiled. "Great."

Once everyone was in the dressing room, Daimon yelled, "Okay, guys, this is it! The first duel of the season! Are you ready?"

"*Yesss*!"

"All hands in!"

We placed our hands in the center of the huddle.

"Duel it on three! One, two, three!"

"*Duel it*!"

"Let's do this!"

We ran onto the field amidst applause and yells of admiration. Calix smiled and waved from the stands, but Carrigan wasn't with him. I scanned the rest of the crowd for Taurik but came up short. His friends were sitting close to my team's bench. When Malicious, Bite, and Cash saw me, they waved enthusiastically. Draegan and Cassius's eyes drooped, as usual.

Catching Malicious' eye, I mouthed, "Where is he?"

She shrugged and mouthed, "I don't know."

When the team reached the bench, I sat close to Malicious so we could talk during the game. After Daimon briefed us on the game plan, a bell resonated throughout the stadium.

"Here we go, guys!" Daimon turned to me. "Loddy, make sure you observe *everything.*"

"Will do!"

Everyone except Meena and me walked to the middle of the field. They all appeared giddy. Kabe, of course, had a huge grin on his face, as did Daimon and Blaze. Melee and Resno weren't grinning, but they bounced up and down, unable to stay still.

The Mackrivoy team also seemed excited, but besides the grinning Asian, they weren't as obvious about it.

"Pair up!" a bass voice yelled over the stadium sound system.

The Aspasian team paired up with their comparable power mates from Mackrivoy. Daimon and Tervik paired up, as did Kabe and the intimidating girl. Melee faced the beautiful Asian. The last two pairings didn't make sense. Blaze was paired with the blond, non-athletic fellow and Resno with the heavyset guy who looked like he could squish Resno with his thumb.

"Meena, why isn't Blaze fighting the big guy?"

"Because she and Jigben—the big guy—are equally matched," Meena said. "Blaze can't do anything that would make a significant difference that would enable her to beat him."

"Oh."

"Resno, on the other hand, can absorb Jigben's brain cells. He will take away most if not all of Jigben's reasoning skills so Jigben won't comprehend that he must defend himself. He'll be helpless, incapable of summoning the strength he's noted for. Ironic, isn't it?"

"I'll say." Her explanation of the strategy made my thought processes seem shallow.

"So what does the blond fellow do? He doesn't seem athletic at all."

"His name is Wren. He's a pain illusionist who, like Resno, depends on mental attacks. He's paired with Blaze because if he fought with Resno, the outcome would be similar to Blaze fighting Jigben."

"Ugh. That sounds . . ."

"Miserable? I'm sure it is. Thankfully, I haven't ever fought him."

"So a pain illusionist is exactly what it sounds like?"

"Yes. Wren creates the illusion of pain within his foe. The pain can range from that of a paper cut to having a body part ripped off."

"Ouch."

"Let's have a clean game from both sides!" the commentator announced. Transparent walls rose inside the field, separating the pairs of duelists from one another. "Duelers ready!" Both teams crouched in fighting position, their expressions focused. "Duel it in three—"

The spectators inhaled collectively.

"Two—"

The spectators held their breath. Then, when

everyone began to accept that the last number wasn't coming, the voice yelled, "One!"

Each pairing sprang into motion. I focused on Blaze and Wren, curious as to how Blaze would beat someone whose power seemed inescapable. Blaze dropped to the ground, her features contorted in pain. "Oh no!" I exclaimed, feeling sorry for her even though she had never been pleasant toward me.

"She's fine, Loddy," Meena said. "The pain isn't real, so it doesn't leave any damage."

As I watched Blaze and Wren, the commentator yelled, "Jigben has been eliminated!" The cheering and clapping were thunderous.

I couldn't look at Resno's sector where Jigben's body had disappeared because I was fixated on Blaze writhing on the ground. "This is horrible! Someone should do something!"

"Just keep watching, Loddy. Blaze was paired with Wren for a reason."

Blaze continued to thrash in pain. When I was sure she was beaten, she steeled herself and got up.

Wren was amazed.

Unhindered by the pain, Blaze ran and punched Wren. He flew backwards, slamming into the wall before his crumpled body landed in a pile on the ground.

"Wow!"

The commentator announced, "Wren has been eliminated!"

The stands erupted in applause and cheering.

"How did Blaze manage that?"

"Blaze is strong physically *and* mentally."

"I see." I wasn't sure if I could have pushed through the pain.

Wren's mangled body disappeared from the field.

"Where did Wren's body go?"

"The field has an appenda-port so the watcher who controls the game can transport the defeated out of each sector."

I looked toward Kabe and the dark-headed girl's sector. Her entire body was covered in spikes and Kabe's in blood. Although he was clearly in pain, he continued to jab at her. When she failed to defend one of his leg blows, Kabe took advantage of her hesitation and knocked her to the ground. Then, grimacing in pain, he grabbed her hands and held her legs down with his knees.

The commentator yelled, "Gianna has been eliminated!"

The yells were boisterous.

I leaned over and shouted to Meena, "The duels aren't long."

"No," she said. "Instant KO's almost always happen at the beginning. As the match progresses, the duels require more effort. Daimon and Tervik's duel may last for another twenty minutes."

I looked in time to see Daimon raise his arm to strike Tervik. A scarlet ring appeared, circling Tervik midair and shooting spikes at Daimon.

"They're evenly matched," Meena said.

"Really?"

"Yes. But Daimon is the only one who has a chance

of beating Tervik."

Melee and the Asian fought using the elements. The Asian manipulated water in midair that, aside from its whipping attacks on Melee, rushed with an appealing fluid motion.

The Asian looked frustrated, though. He would aim the water in a certain direction, but the water would suddenly stop or drop. I couldn't figure it out until I examined Melee. Concentrated light levitated around Melee that, instead of striking her opponent would weave through the water causing the water to stop or drop.

"How fascinating."

"Yes," Meena said, "Watching elementals fight is intriguing."

Taurik scooted next to me. He wasn't supposed to sit on the bench because he wasn't on the duel team, but I couldn't win that fight. "Where have you been?"

"Nowhere special. Why?"

I stared into his eyes to see if he was lying. "I thought you'd be here sooner."

"I was finishing homework, and time got away from me, that's all."

Malicious's and my eyes met. She was suspicious of his story, as was I. He always seemed to be up to something.

"Hey, Taurik," Meena said.

"Hey, Meena. How's the match going?"

"Good so far." She didn't sound like she was flirting with him.

"I bet Daimon will beat Tervik. Tervik seems messy

with his attacks."

Meena shrugged. "He's actually known for being effective despite the messiness."

"What about the other guy fighting Melee? How skilled is he?"

"Avix? His fighting style is different but just as powerful. He's controlled in every sense, and quite graceful—if you haven't noticed."

Taurik smiled. "Oh, I have."

As Meena and Taurik chatted about Mackrivoy's duelists, I leaned back toward Malicious. "Think he told me the truth?"

"I don't know. He didn't tell anyone where he was."

"I'm sure it's nothing."

"Who knows?"

I straightened. Meena and Taurik were discussing Jigben's size. As I shifted my attention back to the duels, I noticed Cannon, arms folded, staring at me from the other side of the field. She probably couldn't stand Taurik's sitting with me.

Melee had created doppelgangers of herself that filled the entire sector, and Avix was assessing his situation. When the copies charged him, a surge of excitement ran through me. *She's going to win.*

But as one of the Melees leaned in to touch him, Avix arched forward, bringing his arms in and ducking his head to create a human cocoon. He appeared to be forming something with his hands. He then broke out of the cocoon, with shards of ice flying in every direction, striking every apparition.

All the illusions disappeared, and the real Melee collapsed in pain. Before she hit the turf, I saw the spattered blood covering her face and body.

Avix raised his hands. He directed the water that sprang up from the field toward Melee's arms and legs.

My heart pounded. "He's not killing her, is he?"

"No," Meena said, "murder isn't allowed."

Water hovered around Melee's hands and feet before transforming into ice. She writhed trying to escape but was unable to free her hands and feet.

"Melee has been eliminated!" The crowd booed while some—obviously from Mackrivoy—clapped and cheered before Melee's body disappeared.

"Oh, no." Distress was clear in my voice. I couldn't believe Melee had been defeated.

"Don't worry," Meena said. "She's the only player we've lost."

"Yeah," Taurik commented, "she deserved it, anyway."

In an attempt to keep things cordial, Meena said, "She *did* put up a good fight."

"What happens now?" I asked.

"Avix will choose his next opponent."

"But Kabe, Resno, and Blaze have been waiting longer."

"The person who wins most recently chooses because his or her opponent requires more effort to beat."

Avix considered each Aspasian competitor. His body rigid, he didn't blink. "I choose Blaze!" Instantly, Blaze was transported into Avix's sector.

"Why did he choose her?" I said.

"Avix knows she's the most difficult competitor, and since he beat Melee so quickly, he has the most energy for the remainder of the match. He's protecting Tervik, too, assuming Tervik beats Daimon. All Tervik's energy is keeping Daimon at bay, so if he opposes anyone stronger than himself after their duel, he'll lose."

I scanned the field for Tervik and Daimon's sector. Tervik was hunched over, looking exhausted, whereas Daimon was restless and fighting with more energy than he'd had at the beginning of the duel.

I shifted my attention back to where Blaze and Avix's duel had already begun. Avix's body was coated with ice that became thicker as Blaze struck it. "Wow."

"Wow is right," Taurik said. "That guy doesn't kid around."

"I'd hate to oppose him," Meena said.

The ice cocoon became more solid until Avix's body couldn't be seen. "What's he doing?"

"He's protecting himself from her blows."

"How can he attack from inside that cocoon?"

"I'm not sure."

I was surprised that, for once, Meena didn't have an answer.

"Tervik has been eliminated!" The crowd rose to its feet and cheered, and I could hardly believe it.

"Yay!" Meena yelled. "It's almost over!"

Blaze continued punching the impenetrable ice fortress, which shook whenever she hit it. Cracks began to form across its surface. The icy cocoon stopped bulging, and Blaze stopped clobbering. Her mixed expression of cluelessness and concentration made me sweat.

We all held our breath. *What was he doing?*

Blaze huffed in annoyance, and she started punching the cocoon harder, but the cracks only widened slightly. "*Ahh*!" Blaze yelled, "Stop *hiding*!" She flew upwards and then descended, her fist readied for another punch. But before she could strike the cocoon, it rose to reveal Avix underneath. The cocoon flipped upside down and shot up to trap Blaze against the ceiling.

Avix, having landed on his feet during the exchange, stared upwards with an indifferent expression. The ice trap muffled the sound of Blaze's punches.

"Oh no." Trepidation was in Meena's voice.

"Blaze can break out, right?"

"Not in the next few minutes."

Avix rolled an imaginary ball in his hands, and the ice became a sphere before he lowered it to the turf.

"What's he doing?" I asked.

"He's probably squishing her," Taurik said. When I looked at him disapprovingly, his smile disappeared.

"I hate to say it, Loddy," Meena said, "but Taurik may be right."

"But he can't *kill* her!"

"No, but he can orchestrate circumstances that almost cause death."

"*What*?" Sheer terror was in my voice.

"Dueling isn't for the faint-hearted."

Avix's fingers closed on the imaginary ball, and the orb of ice shrank. Blaze's shrieks filled the stadium.

"Stop it!" I yelled. Everyone in the stands looked at me, even Avix. I stared into his relaxed eyes before he shifted his attention back to the sphere.

Before Avix could do any more damage, the commentator yelled, "Blaze has been eliminated!"

The Mackrivoy crowd cheered.

"Is she dead?"

"No, Loddy," Meena said, polite annoyance in her voice. "The game-watcher ensures that doesn't happen. Avix forced Blaze's exit."

The time had come for Avix to choose his next opponent. He deliberated for a while, then announced. "I choose Daimon!"

Daimon smiled before he was transported into Avix's sector. He had been hoping to oppose Avix. Watching him, Daimon crouched.

"I'm afraid for Daimon."

"I am, too."

"Daimon will be fine," Taurik said. "He's team captain."

"Being captain doesn't ensure success," Meena said, "especially when fighting Avix."

Daimon ran at Avix and started punching, but Avix dodged every blow. Daimon didn't let up, though. After a while, Avix's energy seemed to wane. Daimon wasn't giving him a second to concentrate on his aquatic ability.

Avix was no longer the confident competitor he had been during his other duels. He began to worry, and with his worry came slip-ups. At first, he only missed leg blows, but as he became more exhausted, he began taking hits to his upper body. When Daimon struck Avix's face, Avix fell to the ground, and Daimon dove to restrain his arms and legs.

Within seconds, the commentator announced, "Avix has been eliminated! Abervania wins!"

The crowd erupted in applause and cheers. "*Abervania*! *Abervania*! *Abervania*!"

Meena and I clutched each other, jumping and shouting. Malicious and Cash grinned and gave me the thumbs-up while Bite cheered. Cassius and Draegan remained seated, but Cassius was beaming.

13

Sleepover

After the match, the team ambled to the dressing room where everyone praised Daimon's beating Avix.

"Thank you, thank you." Daimon snickered.

I was crossing the field on my way to meet Cannon when Calix caught up with me. "Hey, Loddy! Carrigan's sorry he couldn't make it. He got behind with homework."

"Oh, that's okay," I said, but I wondered if that was the real reason.

"I can't wait to watch you duel. Avix won't see you coming."

"I'm far too inexperienced to fight Avix."

"You never know." Calix smiled as if he knew something I didn't. "I have to go. I'll see you tomorrow. Congratulations on the win!"

"Thanks."

I saw Cannon gossiping with the metaprites on the opposite side of the field from Taurik, his friends, and me. I wished I could have gone with Taurik instead of Cannon.

Cash joined me from the gaggle surrounding Taurik. "Ready for the sleepover?"

"You know it."

"You'll be fine. If you hate it, you never have to go back."

"You're right."

Glancing across at Cannon, Malicious said, "Appease the beast soon. She's glaring at us like she's trying to burn holes in our heads."

When I gazed at Cannon, she turned away and resumed talking. I turned back to Cash. "Wish me luck."

"Luck," Cash said. "You're gonna need it."

Taurik separated from his friends, and I hugged him.

He pulled away, staring at me. "Have fun."

"I'll try." I waved to him and his friends before trekking across the field to Cannon.

"Hey, Loddy! I'm so glad you're here. I've been waiting for you. Are you ready?" Cannon chattered.

"Yes," I said, but I wasn't.

"Great! I can't wait to talk about everything! Let's go!"

On our way, Cannon gabbed about the highs of the match. I was surprised she had actually paid attention to the duels. When we arrived in her room, she flopped down on the bed while I sat on the edge, taking in her decorating choices.

The comforter was hot pink, and the walls were lime green. Her closet occupied half the wall, and her heart anthilomy, that visual representation of those she loved, sat in the middle of her humongous dresser. Her vanity was the pink of a Barbie Dreamhouse, filled with a plethora of makeup and hair products and surrounded by lights like those bordering a movie star's mirror.

I expected to see pictures on the walls but came up short. Before I could ponder this, I spotted Taurik in her heart anthilomy. What was funny was that even Taurik's anthilomy-self was repulsed by Cannon. Within her anthilomy, he paced around as if he were in a dungeon.

Cannon shielded the anthilomy with her body. "You weren't supposed to see that." The red in her face became more pronounced every second.

If she wasn't so embarrassed, I would have been angrier. "It's okay. I know you don't have control over the anthilomy."

"But it was inconsiderate of me not to cover it up. I'm *so* sorry."

"It's okay. *Really*."

Cannon glanced into my eyes. Seeing that I was okay with her anthilomy, she sat next to me.

"What really happened between you and Taurik?"

"I told you. He stole my memories."

"I can't believe he would purposely sabotage someone."

"Well, he did." She was defensive, but insincerity permeated her tone.

"Is that what the headmistress wants you to say?" I tried making eye contact, but she avoided my gaze. "Cannon, what *really* happened?"

"Why don't you believe me?"

"Because you're not telling me the whole story."

She bit her lip. "*I'm telling the truth.*"

"Taurik wouldn't deceive you without a good

reason."

Cannon started sweating and blinking profusely. "I—I have to go to the bathroom." She got up and slammed the door behind her.

Talking through the door, I said, "Cannon, you can tell me."

She whispered, "Can't come out now."

Air whooshed. An unfamiliar male voice murmured, "Can't say anything."

Another whoosh of air. "Loddy, I'll be out soon!"

"Is someone in there with you?"

A pause. "No."

"I thought I heard someone."

"No one's here but me." Her voice was tremulous.

"Cannon, please come out and tell me what happened."

"I can't!"

"Yes, you can! *Please*."

After a while, the doorknob turned. Cannon's expression was serious. "He did take a lot of memories, but he didn't mean to take so many."

"I see."

"He only took them because I asked him to."

"Why?"

She began to tear up.

I placed my hand on her shoulder, but she didn't speak. "Cannon?"

She slumped down and began bawling.

I rubbed her back and let her cry.

Finally, her crying subsided and she got up. "I was,

uh, I was abused—by another student."

I couldn't believe it. "Cannon—I don't know what to say."

Her eyes were blank, eyeliner strewn across them. "No one does."

"Who would do—?"

"You wouldn't believe me—along with everyone else at this school." Fresh tears cascaded through her makeup, gathering oil and coloring before running down either side of her face.

"Do I know him?"

"Yes. Everyone *loves* him."

I thought of the duel team. Every student knew the duelists. "Daimon?"

"*Please*. Daimon really is as perfect as people think. He would never—"

My mind flew to Resno before shifting to the guy Taurik had warned me about. "Kabe?"

A new batch of tears commenced. Convulsing, Cannon cried into my shoulder, and everything Taurik had said to me about Kabe made sense. After a while, Cannon composed herself and wiped away her tears.

"Are you okay?"

She shrugged. "I'll be all right. I just haven't visited this in a long time. It feels therapeutic—to finally share it with someone who believes me."

"*No one* believes you?"

"Some people believe me, but they're the same ones who believe it's my fault that I didn't prevent it. The funny thing is, for a while, I thought it *was* my fault. But I see now that it wasn't. I couldn't have stopped him."

I was in utter disbelief. How could I not have known that Cannon had been taken advantage of? How could someone have kept a secret of that magnitude hidden from everyone? "I can't imagine going through that alone. Do your parents know?"

"They don't care."

"Surely they—"

"Nope. They don't. They're too busy living their extravagant lives to deal with something like this. In their world, this kind of stuff doesn't happen to people like us, when in reality, it can happen to *anyone*."

"Oh, Cannon." I hugged her. She accepted it half-heartedly before becoming rigid and uncomfortable, prompting me to retreat from her personal space.

"I can take care of myself."

"But you shouldn't have to all the time, and especially not under these circumstances."

She smiled. "I'm sure you're wondering how Taurik works into my story?"

"You don't have to tell me if you don't want to."

"But I do. The rest is easy to explain."

"Okay."

Nevertheless, she steeled herself and looked into my eyes. "After I cut Kabe out of my life, I asked Taurik to remove all the painful memories so I'd never have to relive them again. He agreed, but the cleanse didn't go as planned."

"Oh, no."

"He intended to only take the painful memories that

involved *Kabe*, but instead, he took different memories."

"Why did he do that?"

"He felt sorry for me after he saw my unpleasant memories involving my parents. He saw the way they treated me at home and how they disregarded me as a daughter, and how they saw me as a burden. So, without consulting me, Taurik took the memories until most of them were all gone. Unfortunately, painful memories are all I have regarding my parents, so—"

"He tried to take everything you could remember about your parents?"

"Exactly. And I know Taurik was trying to help and that my parents aren't wonderful people, but they're still my parents. As if I wasn't isolated enough from them, you know?"

"Yes." I could understand Cannon's story from both sides.

"He apologized so many times. I knew he felt horrible, so I forgave him, and everything went back to normal. I thought we were fine until I talked to the headmistress. She told me that Taurik wasn't innocent and that it was his intention to take those memories all along. She said he liked to prey on people who couldn't tolerate distressing memories, and that I was just his victim.

"Kallisto planted a seed of doubt in my mind that grew until I believed every detail of her story. I started to see Taurik in the worst light. His voice, his mannerisms, his scent—all became unbearable for me. Then one day, I told him I couldn't stand him anymore." Cannon looked down. "Of course, he couldn't understand why his presence had become intolerable. So I told him about the headmistress, and the fight left him.

"Taurik said that if I could believe the headmistress's lie that he didn't care for me, then we couldn't be friends. We've been at odds ever since. But as you saw in my heart anthilomy, I don't see Taurik as an enemy. I just don't trust him."

So Kallisto had succeeded in destroying Taurik and Cannon's friendship. I wasn't sure why she would have wanted to, though. "I can understand why you don't trust Taurik, but I still do. I appreciate your having tried to warn me in the headmistress's office, though."

She stared at me, her expression frozen. "Of course." She got up from the floor to go and stare out a window overlooking the campus.

As I observed her forlorn expression, it occurred to me that Cannon was desolate. "Are you disappointed, Cannon, because I haven't changed my position, because I still trust Taurik?"

"I'm *very* disappointed that you haven't changed your position! Frightened, even."

"Frightened of what?"

Turning from the window, she said, "My story was supposed to influence you to change your stance on Taurik. The headmistress said so."

I finally understood why Cannon was making such a fuss. "So Kallisto put you up to this."

Cannon nodded. "And now I've failed. I'm afraid to learn what she'll do to me."

"I can't say I'm surprised. Has Kallisto ever asked

you to spy on me?"

Cannon's eyes shifted to the ground before she nodded.

"I knew it." So I wasn't paranoid.

"The headmistress worries about you. Please don't tell her I told you; she'd crucify me!"

"I won't tell her if you promise to give me a break from spying once in a while."

"Fine," she said, but nervousness became apparent in her eyes. "There—there's something else you should know."

"What?"

Before she could answer, she dropped to her knees, clutching her stomach and gasping.

I fell to my knees. "Cannon, what's wrong?"

"You—you should—probably leave!"

"I can't leave you like this!"

Alarm filled her eyes. She grabbed my collar and pulled me close. "You *have* to or it won't leave!"

"What won't leave?"

"*Just go!*"

"But, Cannon—"

"Trust me, Loddy. I'll be fine if you just *go now*!"

I stood. Waves wracked through her entire body. She clutched her stomach as if something was eating its way out.

As I closed her bedroom door behind me, she inhaled sharply in pain. I put my ear up to the door. Just as when I had been outside the bathroom door, I heard a whoosh of air, but this time I didn't hear the male voice—

just silence. Then someone made his or her way to the bathroom and closed the door. I knew I wouldn't be able to hear anything through two doors, so I decided to trust Cannon and go back to my room.

As I entered the glass pod, I thought about the voice. I realized that I had heard it many times since being in Aspasia. There was no mistaking it. In fact, it belonged to one of the students who had greeted me on my first day. The voice of the mystery man belonged to Carrigan Peatleaf.

14

SUSPICIONS

I couldn't make sense of Carrigan and Cannon. How could Carrigan have gained entry into Cannon's room without my noticing him? Besides that, why were they together?

I reached my room and saw a piece of paper folded up inside the keyhole. The last person who'd sent me a note was Meda, the guardian of Chaste Palez. What was so important that she had sent another one? Then I realized the message could have been from Professor Omega, and my heart leapt.

I pulled the paper out of the keyhole and took it inside my room. As I unfolded the note, I didn't recognize the handwriting.

Sorry I can't say much, but I assure you. I'm on your side.

Evily

Evily? What could have prompted her to send me such a personal message? The paper began to disappear before I could register it. Within seconds, it was gone.

What was happening? Professor Omega had disappeared and I still didn't know his location. I couldn't ascertain whether Aunt Maggie and Uncle William were still alive because I didn't have my appenda-port, and Kallisto wasn't giving it back. Kallisto and Kesta weren't telling me a secret, and Taurik, the only other person who knew that secret, couldn't tell me because he would lose his life. Cannon had spied on me for Kallisto who wanted to monitor my relationship with Taurik. Could that mean others were spying on me? Finally, I didn't know what my connection was to the Clevists, and neither did I know why two people had pledged their loyalty to me.

The longer I was at Abervania, the more questions piled up, and the more overwhelmed I felt. I couldn't believe I had so many unanswered questions, and the sad part was, I couldn't do anything but wait for events to unfold.

On the weekend, Taurik, Malicious, and I went to Gadley, a renowned restaurant in nearby Vashia. Gadley served food appropriate for any power type and had Bottomless Pits, which pleased Taurik.

Noticing my puzzlement as we examined our menus, Malicious said, "You want the Bowdian soup. It has a smidgeon of everything, so any drink compliments it."

"I'll trust you."

"You won't regret it." Her eyes twinkled.

After we placed our orders, Malicous turned to me. "How was the sleepover?" She glanced at Taurik. "Beat you to it!"

Taurik stuck his tongue out at her.

"The sleepover didn't happen."

Malicious gasped. "No way! Why?"

"We had a heart-to-heart," I said.

Malicious' expression froze. "I don't understand."

"I won't say what she told me—" I made eye contact with Taurik who knew what the topic of our discussion had been— "but she isn't as cold-hearted as she seems. She's human." I paused, thinking about Cannon's tragic story.

Malicious nodded. "But why didn't the sleepover happen?"

I told them about Cannon losing control of her body in the midst of telling me a secret, about how she kicked me out, and about my hearing Carrigan's voice in her room.

"Cash said he's seen Carrigan around the administration building frequently," Malicious added.

"Why would he be in her room, though?"

"I have no idea," Taurik said.

"I didn't see him while I was there. Wouldn't I have seen him in such a small space?"

"That's true," Malicious agreed, "unless he shrunk himself."

"Nope," Taurik said. "He's a plant manipulator, which means he couldn't have gotten into the palez."

"Unless he had inside help," I said.

"It's impossible. Chaste Palez is the most magically reinforced building on campus. If you don't live there, you can't get in."

"But I got *you* in."

"Oh, yeah." Taurik bit his lip, staring off into the distance. "I *still* don't know how you did that. You're the only person I know who's done it."

"Could Cannon have transported Carrigan?" Malicious looked doubtful.

Taurik shook his head. "Surely not."

"It's a mystery," I said.

"Not for long." Mischief was in Taurik's voice.

"What do you mean?"

"I may snoop around."

"Taurik, I don't want you getting into trouble."

"I'll be fine."

"Taurik Night, I forbid you from pursuing Cannon's secret. The headmistress is probably connected, and if she finds out that you're snooping, she'll hurt you."

"You can't forbid me from investigating. You aren't my girlfriend yet, *Loddy Clementine*."

My heart fluttered. Yet—he'd said yet!

Taurik blushed when he realized what he'd said.

"Well, I'm on Loddy's side," Malicious piped up. "You're too involved with the headmistress's affairs."

Relieved that Malicious had saved him from embarrassment, Taurik said, "Looks like I'm getting more involved. By the way, Loddy, when you saw the headmistress, did she return your appenda-port?"

"No."

"Ugh. If you want anything done right in this world, you have to do it yourself."

"Whatever you mean by that sounds dangerous. Please be careful."

The following Monday after quintessence, I was surprised when Cannon awkwardly approached me. She sounded like she was forcing herself to be nonchalant. "So, about the sleepover . . ."

"Yes?"

"I'm sure you're confused about what happened."

"Very."

"I'm not pregnant if that's what you're thinking."

"I wasn't." Surprisingly, that hadn't occurred to me.

"It wouldn't be the first time someone thought I was." That she had become so jaded was sad.

"That thought never occurred to me, Cannon." I touched her shoulder.

She smiled. "Good, because the real reason I kicked you out was so I could spend time with my boyfriend."

She was lying. She couldn't have been dating Carrigan secretly because their personalities were incompatible. "You mean Carrigan?"

Her eyes enlarged in surprise. "Peatleaf?" Her expression melted into disgust. "Eww! Loddy, how could you think that?"

"Because it sounded like he was in your bathroom—and your bedroom—after I left." Cannon stuck her finger in her mouth to imitate vomiting. "*That* is disgusting! *He* is disgusting!"

"Who was in your room?"

She wracked her brain, struggling for a name. "You wouldn't know him. He doesn't run in your circles."

"Really? Then why didn't I see him in your heart anthilomy?"

She struggled to appear calm but failed miserably, as beads of perspiration formed on her brow. "We just started dating."

I was tired of her lies. "What's his name?"

She stared at me blankly. "Brack."

"Brack?"

"Yes."

"What does Brack look like?"

She pretended to be caught in a dream. "Tall, handsome—blue eyes you or any girl could swim in."

"I don't believe it."

She smiled coyly at me. "Okay . . ."

I stared her down. "Cannon, I know you're lying, and I'm going to find out why."

Cannon pretended to glance down at a wristwatch. "Won't you look at the time? I have to get to my next class." She trotted away as I stared after her, eyes narrowed, determined to find out why she would lie to me.

During History of Aspasia, I confronted Carrigan. "Were you in Cannon's room on Friday?"

"*Cannon*?" Carrigan drew back in disgust. "Like I'd be anywhere near *her*."

"But I heard your voice."

"It wasn't me, okay?"

I backed off.

During power practice, Kallisto observed me, but not Sulwen, Evily, or Meena. They had been temporarily transferred to another class to expose other students to chastes. When I asked Professor Pex why I'd been left behind, he said only three were needed to reveal chaste powers to new students, and he wanted me to captain a team in power practice because he thought I knew what I was doing.

Only four of us remained—Calix, Cannon, Blaze, and me. Since two people were on each team, Calix and I paired up to oppose Cannon and Blaze. We discussed our strategy and decided Calix would confuse them with mental conversation while I delivered the final blows.

I was nervous because I was the only one who could deliver the physical power to defeat them, and so far, I had been unsuccessful. I wasn't sure if whatever had hindered me last time was going to prevent me from succeeding again. If so, Calix and I were in trouble.

"Are you okay? What are you going to do?" Calix asked.

"I don't know. I cleared my head last time, but I wasn't able to use the energy I'd summoned. Something prevented me from letting go."

"Really?"

"Yes. So unless you have a mental ability than can stop Blaze from moving, we're probably going to lose again."

"I'm afraid I don't."

"Ah, well. If we lose, we lose. I should be used to it by now."

"Just try your best. That's all you can do."

"Okay." My eyes darted about the room as I twisted a strand of hair around and around and shifted my weight from side to side.

We were thrust into the illusion. Blaze and Cannon

covered their ears, trying to ignore Calix's mental voice. I cleared my head and felt new energy surging inside. But unlike last time, I felt the energy press against every pore of my body.

You accessed our power, didn't you?

The dark phoenix's voice took me by surprise.

Well, go ahead. Strike the blonde idiot. She deserves it!

I still didn't know how to smother the phoenix, but I didn't have time to think. Blaze was running toward me, fists clenched.

I squeezed my eyes shut and concentrated all my energy into my hands. I wasn't sure what was happening, but I knew the energy awaited my permission to be unleashed. So I let go. Heat exploded in Blaze's direction. The red-hot energy struck Blaze at enormous speed. She was on the ground, shielding her face and writhing in agony as the heat permeated her hands and scorched her face and body until her skin began to melt.

I was distraught because I was causing her agony. I almost stopped the heat, but then I reminded myself that we were in an illusion and none of the pain was real.

Keep going! She'll be gone soon!

I strained to ignore the phoenix's voice. That it approved my actions troubled me. Averting my eyes from the screaming Blaze, I repeated *it's just an illusion, it's just an illusion* and unleashed another round.

Finally, Blaze grunted in defeat. Her entire body was scorched, and she wasn't moving.

Such power we have!

The dark phoenix's voice sounded relieved. I could feel its pleasure at having defeated another opponent.

Cannon and Calix were engaged in hand-to-hand combat. When Cannon saw that I had beaten Blaze, the color left her face.

I walked toward them. "Move, Calix."

"No need!" Cannon said, raising her hands in surrender. "I give up!"

"I wouldn't do that just yet."

It couldn't be. The familiar voice was one I hadn't heard in a while. I thought she'd left Abervania for good. "Valisa?"

Grinning darkly, Valisa O'Vain stood a few yards away. "Yeah, it's me. Surprised?"

"A little."

She came nearer. "Loddy, I don't scare easily. My parents, on the other hand, do. They didn't give me a choice when they insisted I leave Abervania, but when I convinced them that they were limiting me after they'd made me transfer, I got my way—as I always do."

"I see." I kept my guard up.

Valisa giggled. "Of course, my parents had a stipulation. I have to be monitored in case you get too close." She stared at the small space between us.

Then, without warning, she attacked. It happened so fast that I couldn't register it until I was on the ground. When I felt her hair uncoil from my leg, I realized it must have slithered up from behind. I got up.

Calix was down and Valisa, looking triumphant, was standing over him. Cannon was watching Valisa in awe.

"Valisa," I said, "we'll catch up later." At the sound of my voice she turned. I shot heat at her and Cannon, giving Calix time to crawl away.

Valisa's hair shielded her and Cannon. Surprisingly, her hair didn't burn.

I turned to Calix. "I don't understand. Is her hair invincible?"

"It's composed of different fibers that make it impervious to heat."

"Of course it is." Unsure of what to do, I continued blasting the red-hot energy at Valisa and Cannon. "How do we beat her?"

"Can you utilize another power type?"

"I've never used anything other than fire."

"I'm sure you can use any power type considering you woke every conversion stone."

"But I don't know how to access other abilities."

Valisa and Cannon started closing in on us.

"Just concentrate on a different power and let it go."

To call on an ability my body wasn't accustomed to using was intimidating. I started sweating as I wracked my brain for the unique powers to which I'd been exposed. Quickly I settled on Avix's water manipulation. I concentrated, trying to envision a water-controller's mind. I tried being calm and calculating like Avix.

The dark phoenix started laughing.

"What's so funny?"

You can't control water, sweetie.

"Why not?"

Ask the headmistress. She'll have an answer.

"Loddy, who are you talking to?" Calix asked.

"Tell you later."

Valisa and Cannon, who had gotten dangerously close, were staring at me with confused expressions.

I tried intensifying the heat. When that didn't work, I widened the flame so that it stretched beyond the hair's reach, but the hair extended along with it. My shoulders slumped. "I can't do it."

"Plan B?"

"I don't have one."

Closer, closer—Valisa and Cannon were within two feet of us!

"We need to do something *now*!" Calix yelled.

The dark phoenix laughed in the background.

Then inspiration hit. "She controls the hair with her mind, right?"

"Yes!"

"So hack into that mental connection!"

"Between her and her hair?"

"Yes!"

"I've never done that before, but here goes."

They were as close as they could be without touching us.

I was about to accept defeat when Valisa grunted from behind the flames. Her hair moved out of the way long enough for me to strike. Her scream was piercing. Within seconds, she was defeated.

At the same time, Calix beat Cannon to the ground.

As the illusion melted, I realized we had won. I

looked around the gym for Kallisto, but she was gone.

Beaming, Professor Pex strolled toward Calix and me. "Loddy Clementine, you've done it!"

"*We* did it, sir!" I made eye contact with Valisa who still looked surprised. Then she slumped into the dressing room with Cannon and Blaze.

Professor Pex forced himself to address Calix's contribution, "Outstanding! You've both come a long way!"

"Thank you, sir," Calix said.

"Professor, where did the headmistress go?"

"She had to leave campus. She said she can't attend after-school lessons today."

"Okay." I wasn't sure if I was being paranoid, but I wondered if she had caught my conversation with the dark phoenix and left so she didn't have to answer my question about the parameters of my power.

"Who were you talking to during the match?" the Professor asked curiously.

"Talking to?" Oh, no. I made eye contact with Calix, and at that moment he understood that during the match it was the dark phoenix with whom I'd been conversing.

"Yes. The conversation you and Calix were, uh, discussing."

"Oh! I was talking to myself." I looked to Calix for help with embellishing the story.

Calix joined in. "Oh, yeah. She does that a lot."

Professor Pex glanced at Calix.

"She talks to herself to cope with anxiety," he

added.

I nodded.

The Professor paused. “Works for me!”

Calix and I exhaled.

15

BOILING POINT

When I came out of the dressing room, Calix was waiting. "Have Valisa and her crew left?" I asked.

"Yes."

I probably wouldn't be alive if all the girls shared the same dressing room.

As we left the gym, Calix asked, "What *were* you discussing with the phoenix?"

"It told me that I wouldn't be able to manipulate water, which was what I had planned to use instead of fire."

"Why wouldn't you be able to manipulate water?"

"I don't know. The phoenix told me to ask the headmistress."

"I didn't think you were supposed to talk to it."

"How did you know that?" I couldn't remember telling him about my conversations with the headmistress.

"You told me," he said, his expression neutral. "Remember?"

"No."

"Really?"

He seemed so at ease, he couldn't have been hiding anything, but I was still suspicious. "You haven't been talking to the headmistress, have you?" I joked.

He smiled. “Of course not.”

When we passed the administration building, I felt the urge to talk to Kallisto about the dark phoenix, so I slowed down.

“What are you doing?”

“I’m going to talk to Kallisto about the phoenix.”

“But Pex said she left campus.”

“She may not have left yet. Would you get me in? I’m still without an appenda-port.”

“Sure,” he said, but his voice was apprehensive. He walked slowly toward the appenda-port receiver. “Take my hand.”

I held his hand as he inserted his appenda-port into the metallic hole to transfer us into the building. Once inside, we saw only a few people working, which was different from the swarm of activity I’d observed on my first day.

I walked to the red metallic hole which would transport us to the headmistress’s office and stopped. I looked back at Calix who had not moved since being inside. “Come on!”

“Loddy, I don’t think I should be with you when you ask her about your powers.”

“You don’t have to stay. Just help me get into her office and you can leave.”

“Okay.” Reluctantly, he grabbed my hand and transported both of us to the headmistress’s office.

The room was vacant. Even the cancellers were not present.

“She isn’t here.”

"So let's go."

"Wait. My appenda-port's here." I walked to her desk.

"Loddy, it wouldn't be in her office." Calix looked around nervously. "Her port is on. O don't know why she'd leave it on if she wasn't here, so let's just go before she comes back."

"Would you stop worrying?" I went behind her desk and examined the drawers. "You won't get in trouble if she walks in."

"Yes, I will because I got you in! I'm an accomplice!"

I searched for a drawer handle, but came up short. Appenda-port slots were on the right side of the desk. Great. "Um, Calix?"

"Yes?"

"I need an appenda-port to get into her desk. Do you think you could—"

"No way! I am *not* breaking into the headmistress' desk! It probably requires her appenda-port, anyway."

"You're right." Kallisto stood in the doorway with Kesta and the cancellers. She didn't look happy.

Calix's face turned white.

I stared at Kallisto. "I thought you left campus."

"Save it." Kallisto turned to Kesta. "Make sure Mr. Raze is properly escorted out while I speak with Miss Clementine."

"Yes, ma'am." Kesta escorted Calix out of the office, and the cancellers resumed their positions.

Kallisto strode over to me. She stared, hatred burning in her eyes. Then my head snapped as her palm whipped my cheek.

I clasped the searing flesh. The pain concentrated below my left eye before it spread to the rest of my face. I wouldn't give her the satisfaction of seeing me cry even though tears accumulated in the corners of my eyes.

"I don't understand. I take you in, I bring you to my wonderful school, and I even train you. And this is how I am repaid?"

I squared my shoulders to stare at her with unwavering eyes.

"And you *continue* to associate with that *scum* even though I told you not to." Flames darted in her eyes before she crossed her arms and strode to stare out the window.

"Where is my appenda-port?"

She turned back, flames still flashing in her eyes. "I was about to return it to you before you broke into my office."

"No you weren't."

The flames became more pronounced. "*Excuse* me?"

"You don't want me to have it. Why can't I have it? It's *my* appenda-port."

She considered her words before speaking. "I thought Taurik would try to take you away from me."

I knew it. "But why would I leave you?"

"Because he might try to convince you that your aunt, uncle, and Zander are still alive, and that you should go with him to find them. Am I right?" She peered at my expression and noted my body language.

"No." I blinked rapidly.

"You lie."

I stared at her. I couldn't say anything without making my situation worse.

She came closer, her face inches from mine. "I hate that it's come to this, but I see now that Taurik is the only way to get through to you."

"Leave him alone!"

"I will—provided you never talk to him again." She shrugged. "Otherwise, he might meet with an unfortunate accident."

She had beaten me. I couldn't bear to live without Taurik. I had to leave him alone. "Fine," I said, my voice low. "I won't have anything to do with him." I still had his friends, though.

"Nor his friends."

I hated her. "Nor his friends."

"And you will not inform them of this conversation except to say that you are done with them."

"Fine."

"Repeat it back to me." She was enjoying my pain.

"And I will not inform his friends of this conversation except to say that I am done with them."

"Good. And I am cancelling your lessons. Clearly you don't appreciate them as you should. You may go, Miss Clementine." She smiled. "We're done."

"Why did you leave campus?"

Speaking through clenched teeth, she said, "*We're done*."

I turned to leave, still feeling the stinging pain on my cheek. I remembered the other reason I had come into the administration building in the first place. "I have one more confession to make."

"Yes?" She almost spat the word.

"I've been talking to the dark phoenix."

Kallisto stiffened. "And?"

"And it told me something *fascinating* today."

"And what was that?"

"The phoenix said that I could only access fire, no other power type. When I asked why that was, it said to ask you. What was it talking about?"

She was silent—probably bristling. Finally, she spoke. "No idea."

"Okay. I just had to check. I guess the phoenix is a liar."

Every word calculated, she said, "I suppose it is."

"I *hate* liars."

16

SHORTAGE

I walked to school the next day, hoping I wouldn't see Taurik or his friends. I planned to postpone speaking to them as long as possible. Thankfully, I got to quintessence without meeting any of them. Once seated, I noticed a shortage of students in the class. I turned to Cannon. "Where is everyone?"

"I'll tell you after class."

I wasn't able to listen to Professor Biv's most elaborate entranx lesson thus far because I was preoccupied with the lack of students. After the lecture ended, I turned to Cannon again, bursting with curiosity. "So?"

"It's the beginning of Meda's Week."

"As in *the* Meda, the one who founded Chaste Palez?"

"Yes. The holiday celebrates her contributions to Aspasian society. People celebrate by travelling to her quasian to hear her speak. Parades and feasts follow all week long during which Meda grants gifts to lucky Aspasians. The most fascinating is the gift of herself. She grants 100 chastes the opportunity to visit with her at her home during the week.

"Unfortunately, no one's sure if she's going to

show. The brains haven't been seen in weeks. The celebrations will still commence, though. I'm just happy the headmistress is letting the chastes from Abervania attend this year."

"What do you mean 'this year'?"

"In the past, the headmistress didn't let anyone leave for Meda's Week, but this year, she's allowing chaste students the entire week off so they can celebrate with their families."

"Really!" To put others before herself sounded uncharacteristic of Kallisto.

"Yes. *I* won't leave because I can't stand to be around my family. They probably don't want to see me anyway."

I felt sorry for Cannon because I sensed that she wanted to see her family even though they were abusive. I didn't think I would be leaving campus, either, as long as Kallisto had her eye on me.

When I walked into logic class, I thought how Borjaf had overstayed his welcome. As a student, I strove to listen to everything an instructor said, but in logic, I stared past Borjaf and drowned out his voice. Looking around, I saw a shortage of chaste students as in my previous class.

The same was true in History of Aspasia where Carrigan stood on the opposite side of the room from me. I assumed he didn't want to be barraged with questions about the sleepover.

Yttira began talking about the Flares again, a subject I found riveting. I then recalled the Flare he'd discussed who had gone missing recently. I thought it odd that his location was still unknown. "Professor Yttira?"

"Yes, Miss Clementine?"

"Before you begin your lecture, could you expand on the Flare who went missing recently?"

"Of course. What is your question?"

"What is his name, and exactly how long has he been missing?"

"His name is Zander—"

My heart skipped a beat.

"—and he's been missing for seven years."

Seven years? The last remnants of hope I had to find Zander fled my being. He couldn't be the Zander I knew. My Zander had gone missing just three months ago. Wait a minute! Time is different here. A day on Earth was a month in Aspasia. That meant seven years here was only three months on Earth. "What do you think happened to him?"

"Well, before he went missing, Prince Zander was planning an expedition outside the Aspasian galaxy. He wanted to study a secret project, but no one knows what. After his parents approved his travel, young Zander left without telling anyone where he was going or what he was looking for. At first, his father dismissed his absence as rebellion, but as the days passed, Alexander started to worry. He eventually sent search teams all over Aspasia, but no one found a trace of him. Some believe that Deo had kidnapped him to use him as leverage in the war. He'd kidnapped one of Alexander's children before, so who's to say he hadn't repeated himself?

"It was determined that Deo didn't have the prince in his possession, but old wounds had been reopened and the war got uglier. Now, seven years later, we still have no leads. However, if Prince Zander is outside the Aspasian galaxy, he may not want to be found."

I skipped consummation so that I wouldn't see Taurik or his friends and ate lunch in my room. I wrapped up half my meal because I hated eating alone. I headed to chastology earlier than usual where Evily and I were the only students in the chastology classroom.

"Hmm, now what can I do with two students?" Professor Wakepetal assessed Evily and me. He cocked his head and thought. "Aha! I have an idea!"

Oh, no.

Motioning to the desk next to me, Professor Wakepetal said, "Evily, would you sit next to Loddy, please?"

Evily stared at him with an expression that struggled to appear neutral to conceal her disgust. She marched to the desk and plopped down. She didn't look at me, and I avoided looking at her.

"I want you two to discuss each other!" He smiled showcasing as many teeth as was possible.

My eyes enlarged while Evily fidgeted uncomfortably.

"Today is not about academics! Today is about socialization! Now, I'm going to leave the room, but I'll be back—soon. Toodles!" He waved as he floated out of the room.

I was terrified. I'd never had an actual one-on-one

with Evily. I didn't even know what to discuss. Wait. "I—I got your note."

"Good." She didn't look at me.

"I didn't understand it."

Her voice quavered with trepidation. "I—I can't explain."

"Why not?"

She bit her lip as her eyes darted about the room. "I just can't."

I moved in closer, and she didn't move away. "Evily, what do you know that I don't?"

She closed her eyes.

"What is it? Please tell me. Ever since I've been at Abervania, questions have piled up, but I don't have any answers."

Evily opened her eyes. She trembled as she opened her mouth and closed it. "She—she has Professor Omega."

"What? You mean Kallisto? Are you sure?"

Evily nodded. "She's been keeping him in the basement of her house, and she barely feeds him."

"No!"

"I've been monitoring him. Whenever someone checks on him, I also slip into the house to make sure he's alive."

"How do you go unnoticed?"

"It doesn't matter. What matters is that you two were chummy. He walked you to consummation on your first day."

"That's right. Why does it matter that we're friends, though?"

"Since Cato is his brother, the professor knows how the royal families operate."

"And?"

"And this made the headmistress uneasy for you to be around him."

"Why?"

"You'll see soon enough. After I realized she was uneasy over your friendship, I watched the professor. That day that you and he decided to meet privately, he was abducted from his home and taken to hers. The next day, she told everyone he'd gone on an 'extended leave for an indefinite amount of time' because he 'wasn't feeling like himself.' Sound familiar?"

"Yes." I couldn't believe what I was hearing. "We have to do something!"

Loss sounded in her voice. "What *can* we do, Loddy? No one would believe that a headmistress kidnapped one of her own staff members. Besides, her entire team is in that house at all times, and I can't perform a spell strong enough to transport him out. I'm not Meda."

"I guess we'll just have to wait for an opportunity to rescue him. How much longer do you think he can last?"

"We may get our chance sooner than you think."

"What do you mean?"

Evily looked around. "Kallisto's forcing me to leave."

"She can't do that."

"She can if she caught me spying on Professor Omega."

"No!" I was terrified for Evily because Kallisto was

ruthless. "What did she say?"

"She told me not to tell anyone what I'd seen."

"That's it?"

Evily paused. "She also told me that I was to disappear from campus the moment she said. Otherwise, she would do something unspeakable to my parents."

Evily was risking her parents' and possibly her own safety by telling me about Kallisto's threats. She had been not only an ally but a friend all along.

"Evily, I don't know what to say."

"It's okay. I just hope you understand now how important it is that I don't speak to you." She looked into my eyes. The fear in hers had melted away, replaced by resoluteness.

"Of course. I won't say anything."

"Thank you. If you stay in Vashia instead of going out with the other chastes for Meda's Week, you'll have an opportunity to save Professor Omega. Kallisto is planning something big that she doesn't want to chance the chastes ruining."

"I don't doubt it."

"Loddy, the chastes' powers counteract the dark phoenix. That's why she didn't want me to monitor you, and that's why she forced the chastes in power practice to leave the day our team won."

"It all makes sense."

"You're right, Loddy. She's this galaxy's biggest threat. I just don't know what she's planning. Whatever it is," Evily leaned toward me, "*don't let her win.*"

"I won't."

But I knew exposing Kallisto would be easier said than done.

17

GOODBYE

I hadn't seen Taurik or his friends all day. I was glad, but I knew I couldn't avoid them much longer.

In power practice, Valisa and Blaze straggled up to me, their heads down.

"Loddy." Respect was in Valisa's voice for once.

"Valisa."

"I realize that what happened a few weeks ago wasn't your fault, so—I forgive you for almost killing me."

"Thank you."

"And—you performed well yesterday. Just don't get used to beating me."

"Of course."

She leaned in to inches from my face. "Don't get used to my kindness, either. I still don't like you. I just believe in giving credit where it's due."

There she was, the Valisa I knew. "I wouldn't expect anything more."

She smiled, then walked in the direction of the dressing rooms.

Once Valisa was out of earshot, Blaze whispered, "We're having duel practice after school."

"Thanks! I'll be there."

She grinned and followed Valisa into the dressing room. Valisa and Blaze may not have declared their outright loyalty, but at least they respected me. That was good enough.

I almost skipped aphotology because Taurik and his friends were in the class. My heart pounded as I approached the door to the classroom. As I walked in, dread overtook me. Without thinking, I began chewing on the already raw skin edging my thumbnail. Head down, I took my seat before stealing a glance around. None of them had arrived. Seconds later, they ambled in together except for Malicious and Cash.

Taurik sat next to me. "Hey!"

"Hey." I avoided eye contact.

"Where have you been all day?"

"I'll—I'll tell you after class." I could feel his eyes searching my face.

"Okay," he said, his tone unsure.

I couldn't concentrate during class as a gnawing pain overtook my stomach. That Kallisto was cutting me off from the person who inhabited my every thought wasn't bad enough. She was also cutting me off from his friends, from extensions of him, his ideas and his love.

The end of class came too soon. As I got up, I could feel Taurik's eyes watching me, following me. I almost started to cry, but I steeled myself. I could cry as much as I wanted in my room. My heart sank even further when I discovered Bite, Draegan, and Cassius waiting for us outside the classroom.

"Hi, Loddy!" Bite's smile would have been contagious under any other circumstances. I forced myself to smile. "Hi, Bite." I wondered if Bite could understand the distance I was about to drive between us.

Draegan and Cassius nodded.

Taurik took my hand. "So where have you been all day?"

I pulled my hand away, and my heart ached. Taurik tried making eye contact, but I dodged his efforts.

"Loddy, what's wrong?" Alarm crept into his voice.

I hated that his friends were watching, but their presence made it easier for me to stifle the tears in front of Taurik. "I . . . I can't talk to you anymore."

The alarm in his voice turned to anger. "What do you mean?"

"I . . . I can't associate with any of you."

Everyone processed my words with concentrated expressions.

Taurik's jaw set. "This is *her* idea, isn't it?"

"I don't understand." Bite looked confused.

I made eye contact. "Bite, I really like you. But right now, we can't be around each other for your safety and mine."

"We can't be friends?"

I bit my lip to stop the tears. "No."

"No!" The tears forming in Bite's eyes made him look like a child. He dropped to the ground and began pounding it. "*I like Loddy! I like Loddy! I don't want her to go away!*"

My tears broke through my defenses, but I couldn't

let Taurik see. "I have to go. Goodbye." Before hurrying away, I made eye contact with Draegan and Cassius whose brows were furrowed.

Even when I should have been out of earshot, I could still hear Bite's cries. They tore at me, and although I wouldn't have thought it possible, I hated Kallisto even more. As I was about to exit the building, a hand touched my shoulder. I turned, expecting to see Taurik.

"Draegan." I wiped my tears away. "I'm sorry. I need to go."

"Taurik loves you." His blood red eyes radiated genuineness instead of their usual blankness.

I couldn't speak. That Draegan had let his defenses down was paramount.

Draegan spoke quietly. "You don't have to explain yourself. I know the headmistress is forcing you to cut ties with us in exchange for Taurik's life."

I opened my mouth, but he cut me off with his upraised hand.

"I just want you to know how much he cares for you."

I wracked my brain for something safe to say, but decided it was best to say nothing. We stared at each other before I left. I trudged to my room, bristling at the knowledge that someone had more control over my life than I did, and that that someone was Kallisto Tempest.

18

CHANGE

Before reaching Chaste Palez, I remembered I had duel practice. By the time I walked into the Grobe, I'd wiped away most of the tears.

My teammates were already separated into groups and practicing their combinations. Daimon was directing Meena as Kabe prepared to "attack" her. As I watched Kabe, how I wished I could make him pay for what he had done to Cannon.

Valisa and Blaze were engaged in hand-to-hand combat. Repeatedly, Valisa's hair would crawl toward Blaze and trip her, but Blaze always got up, prepared for another go.

Melee wasn't around, so Resno was by himself, surveying his surroundings. Then Melee appeared, taking swipes at him as he dodged her every move.

As if on cue, they all looked at me with curious expressions.

His voice tentative, Daimon asked, "Is everything okay?"

I nodded.

"Do you feel like practicing?"

"Of course."

"Okay. Well, you can be my partner today since everyone else is paired up."

"That's fine."

"Go change, and we can get started."

Taurik

Fuming, I charged into the Dragon Lady's office. I didn't care if she was preoccupied or not. She was going to listen.

"Hello, Mr. Night." Her voice was snide. She thought she'd already won.

"So now you've barred her from talking to me *and* my friends?"

She didn't look up. "I had to take necessary measures."

"We're her support group!"

"She has more than enough friends."

"Who? Your spies?"

She stared at me. "My spies?"

"Carrigan and Cannon. You're using them, aren't you?"

"I have no idea what you're talking about."

I stepped forward, my hands on her desk, leaning toward her. "Loddy told me about hearing Carrigan's voice in Cannon's room. I'm sure you know about that?"

Her eyes were unblinking. "I don't."

"Right," my jaw set, "Because you don't know anything about what occurs at this school."

Her teeth clenched. "I don't like your tone, Mr. Night."

"And you don't know what happened to Professor Omega, do you? You probably had him murdered because he knows who Loddy is, and you were afraid he'd tell her."

Jumping to her feet, she yelled, "*That is enough*!" Flames spewed on either side of her desk. "You've become too comfortable speaking to me however you wish, Mr. Night."

"I'm going to tell Loddy who she really is!"

She came within inches of my face. "*You wouldn't dare.*"

"I would."

Flames swam in her eyes. "You know what would happen."

"It'd be worth it if it meant bringing you down."

"I hate that it's come to this, Taurik, but I can't let you ruin my plan. *Now*!"

Excruciating pain pierced the back of my head then shot through my body. Dizziness engulfed me before blackness rushed in.

Loddy

When duel practice ended, Daimon told me that our next match would be on Friday against Vainbalt. I was relieved that I had been paired with Daimon who didn't pry into my personal life.

As I left the Grobe, Meena approached me. "Are you okay?"

I nodded, forcing a smile.

"Want to talk about it?" she whispered.

"No."

"Do you need anything?"

"No, just to be alone." Realizing I may have sounded unappreciative, I added, "But thanks for the support."

She tilted her head sympathetically. "No problem."

I continued on my way to Chaste Palez.

"Loddy!" Kabe joined me. "Are you okay? You seemed out of it in practice."

"No. I just need to be alone. But thank you." I turned to leave, but he grabbed my arm.

"Is there anything I can do? Taurik isn't mistreating you, is he?"

He had said his name. That made it worse. "No." I was becoming angry over being confined in a conversation I wanted to end.

"What is it? Look at me."

I saw hunger in his eyes. He yearned for me to say that Taurik had abused me. "I can't talk about it, Kabe."

"Why not?"

"The matter doesn't concern you. Now, let go."

His grip became tighter. "He hurt you, didn't he?"

"No, Kabe. Now, *let go*!"

"I don't understand why you even dated him over me." His grip became so tight that I began to lose circulation.

That was all I could take. I directed heat toward his hand, making sure it was focused on that one spot where he would feel the full impact.

"*Ow*!" He reeled from the scald. "You did that on purpose!"

"That's right. Just like you purposely hurt Cannon and countless others."

He stopped, then struggled to feign confusion. "What are you talking about?"

"Stop acting like you're innocent, Kabe! I know you took advantage of all those girls!"

He stared, processing my words. "You believe I'd do something like that?"

"Yes." I stood resolutely, meeting his gaze.

"I thought you trusted me."

"I did."

His eyes shifted to my lips. He grabbed my shoulders and forced his lips onto mine.

I waited for fire to gather behind every pore of my body before I released it.

Kabe screamed as his clothes burst into flames. In agony, he dropped and rolled on the ground to extinguish the fire.

I grabbed his collar, forcing him to look at me. "You *will* treat every girl with respect, or I'll come after you. Understand? This heat is *nothing* compared with what I wanted to use."

Kabe nodded, choking back his screams.

At that moment, Daimon came out of the stadium with the team. Everyone but Valisa was concerned as they examined Kabe's burns. She looked amused.

"Kabe, are you okay?" Daimon asked.

Kabe looked away.

"Loddy, what's going on?"

I had to be honest. "Kabe tried to take advantage of me, so I burned him."

"No!" Kabe shouted, still writhing in pain. "She attacked me after I turned her down for a date!"

Valisa rolled her eyes, but Daimon and the team looked conflicted. Daimon looked from me to Kabe and shook his head. "I don't know who to believe."

"Believe me!"

As Daimon stared at Kabe, realization dawned on him. He spoke slowly. "This isn't the first time this has happened, Kabe."

Kabe looked offended, then leapt up. "What are you talking about?"

"This isn't the first time that a girl has claimed that you—you took advantage."

"I take what I want. Since when is that a bad thing?"

Daimon surveyed Kabe as if seeing him for the first time. "Not respecting boundaries is a bad thing," he said quietly. Then anger overtook his features. "So all those stories about you were true—and *I defended you*!"

Kabe's innocent façade melted. "They *aren't* true. Those girls lied about what happened." He tried making eye contact with Daimon but failed.

"Are you saying *fifteen* girls lied?"

Fifteen? Wow.

"I haven't dated that many girls in my life."

"Stop lying, Kabe!"

They stared at each other with animosity. I thought they were going to start fighting.

"I'm not lying! But don't expect me to stick with a captain who doesn't trust his best friend!" Kabe cursed and stomped away.

"I wasn't letting you stay anyway!" Daimon called after him. Then he turned to me. "I'm sorry, Loddy."

"I'll be fine."

"I hate it took this long for me to recognize Kabe for what he is. Other girls have approached me about him." He glanced at Valisa. "I've just known him for so long. He was my first friend at Abervania."

"He fooled us all. At least justice has been served, and a lot of other girls will be saved."

"Once the student body knows he's off the team, they'll know the truth." Valisa smiled.

Although I was gratified that Kabe had been exposed, as I walked to Chaste Palez, my world began to collapse around me. When would I be able to talk with Taurik and his friends? Would I be able to rescue Professor Omega? Would I ever see Aunt Maggie and Uncle William again? And what about Zander? How did I feel about him?

Still, despite the tears, knowing that I'd saved girls from experiencing at least one toxic, physically abusive relationship, helped me sleep soundly that night.

19

Time to Act

On Friday, not a single chaste roamed the campus except for Cannon, Meena, Melee, and me. I looked around nervously. I hated to think what Kallisto had in mind for the dark phoenix.

To add to my consternation, Taurik, Malicious, and Cash were absent from both consummation and aphotology.

When I had arrived at chastology, Professor Wakepetal's body tensed. "Miss Clementine, the headmistress wants to speak with you in her office."

I turned to leave.

"And Miss Clementine—"

"Yes?"

He hesitated, and then forced a smile and said, "Have a good day." But his enthusiasm was constrained.

I made eye contact. "You, too, Professor Wakepetal."

A while later, I found Kesta standing outside the administration building.

She lit up when she saw me. "Are you ready?" She extended her hand toward me.

I nodded and took her hand. "What does Kallisto want?" I asked as she led me inside the administration building.

"I'd rather not say." She positioned herself in front of the office appenda-port. "She'll fill you in."

Kallisto stood facing the window beside her desk, staring into space, her jaw set, as if contemplating a disconcerting thought. Pilmus and the other cancellers' were still, but their eyes were bulging out of their heads.

"Loddy. How are you?" Kallisto's voice lacked emotion.

I decided to skip the small-talk. "Taurik and his friends have disappeared. Is this your doing?"

Kesta watched Kallisto and me intently, looking from one to the other and back again.

"I may know what happened to Taurik, but the disappearance of his friends is a mystery. I was going to ask you where they are."

My blood began pumping at an alarming rate. "What did you do to Taurik? Is he alive?"

"Calm yourself. Taurik is fine. Are you sure you don't know where his friends are?"

"*Yes, I'm sure; now where is he*?"

Frustration flashed across her face, but her nonchalance was chilling. "I can't say just yet."

"*Where is he? What do you want*?"

Her eyes narrowed. "The time has come for you to snatch the attention of very important people."

I frowned. "What do you mean?"

Her smile was dark. "Some powerful people are

attending today's duel, and afterwards, they're coming to my house for a reception. You're going to meet them."

So I would be in her house where Professor Omega was being held. Evily was right about my opportunity to rescue him. "Who are these people?"

"You'll see."

"I'm tired of not knowing. *Who are they?*"

She cocked her head. "Someone needs to learn manners."

"I'm waiting." I surprised myself at my assertiveness.

Her dark smile became more pronounced. "Who do you think you are?"

"I think I'm the person you need to execute this plan."

She looked as if she was seeing me for the first time. "Don't forget that I have Taurik, and if I wish, he can be executed."

I stared back with steel in my eyes and said nothing.

"That's what I thought. As I said, you will meet the distinguished guests and gain their trust. Then, when I give the signal, you will act as my leverage as I voice my requests to them."

"How do I do that?"

She grinned, evil glistening in her eyes. "You're going to kill them if they don't give me what I want."

She actually wants me to kill people? My heart raced, and sweat trickled down my neck.

"Something wrong?"

I spoke in a low voice. "You want me to murder

people I don't know?"

"Yes." Her pupils dilated.

"Are they gods?"

She leaned so close that I could smell the garlic she'd had at consummation. "All will be revealed at the match."

"Fine. May I go?"

"Yes. Just act like everything is normal."

"I've been doing that since I got here."

"Then this should be nothing new for you. Kesta, please escort Loddy out."

"Yes, ma'am!" I had forgotten about Kesta.

"And Loddy?"

"Yes, Mother?"

Anger flashed in her eyes. "This conversation never happened."

"Never."

Without looking at Kesta, I exited the administration building.

How am I going to kill innocent people? Maybe they'll give in to Kallisto's demands, and I won't have to. But the way my life was going, I didn't see that happening.

For the rest of the day, I pretended like everything was normal. I didn't tell anyone about my conversation with Kallisto, not even Calix or Carrigan. I would have been tempted to tell Malicious, but since I didn't know where she was, that was impossible. I wondered if Taurik was being held in Kallisto's house with Professor Omega.

After class, I rushed to Chaste Palez to change into my duel clothes. As I walked in, I thought I saw Carrigan entering the glass pod, but I wasn't sure because his back was to me. I ran to the pod as its Torggler door began closing—just in time to confirm that the figure was Carrigan.

I imagined the pod flying toward Cannon's room and depositing Carrigan before coming back for me. But instead of going to my room, I would go to Cannon's. Within seconds, I heard the glass pod hit the ground as it returned. I used my sitzoscope to illuminate the pod, then stepped inside and yelled Cannon's room number.

My heart pounded. *What will I say when I confront them together? What are they trying to hide?*

The glass pod stopped in front of her room. I knocked and waited. Within seconds, I heard someone walking toward the door, murmuring something. The door opened.

"Hey!" Cannon's expression was relaxed.

"May I come in?" I had never sounded so timid.

"Sure!"

As I entered the room, I scanned the entire place without pretense.

"Loddy, what are you doing?"

I searched the bathroom for Carrigan. He wasn't there. How had she hidden him? I studied her face for a sign of alarm but came up short. "Where is he?"

"Where's who?"

"Carrigan."

"Carrigan?" She looked perplexed. "Why would *he* be here?"

"Because I saw him in the glass pod, and he looked

surprised to see me. Where else would he have gone? Every other chaste is home for Meda's Week."

"Wait. He was in *Chaste Palez*? That's impossible."

"Don't lie to me, Cannon."

"I'm not."

"Yes, you are. But it's okay. I'm not going to force it out of you. Most of my life is secrets at this point anyway." I began to leave, but she grabbed my arm. Shame filled her eyes. "Loddy, I wish I could tell you the truth, but I can't. I'm sorry."

So Kallisto had gotten to her, too. As I went to my room, I saw how Kallisto had become the dictator of my life. She dictated how I acted, my relationships, my schedule, my privacy, and my morals. If I wanted my freedom again, she had to be beaten—and I had to be the one to do it.

20

SURPRISE

As soon as I'd changed, I sprinted to the stadium where Daimon was on the field, stretching.

"Hey, Loddy," he said, his voice less enthusiastic than usual.

"Hey." I started stretching along with him. We were silent, and I realized this would be our first duel without Kabe. "How are you?"

"Good. It's just hard," he said, "You think you know someone."

"Yeah." I didn't know what else to say.

"I've always been taught to respect girls, and then Kabe abuses them without any remorse. My closest friend!"

I couldn't believe what I was about to say. Placing my hand on his, we made eye contact. "You can still be his friend."

"No way!" Daimon reeled away. "I can't be associated with him. I'm surprised you of all people would advocate for it. He went after you."

"I know. But, Daimon, don't you think Kabe needs you during his time of greatest weakness?"

His expression softened as he processed my words. “I never thought of Kabe’s situation that way.”

“Sometimes, God is the only one who understands our faults.”

At that moment, Meena and Resno walked into the stadium. Daimon and I waved.

“Hey, guys!” Resno shouted.

“Time to get started,” Daimon called. Turning to me, he added, “I appreciate the talk.”

“Anytime.”

For the next half hour, Daimon prepped everyone on our opponents. Vainbalt’s team consisted of only three players, but they were ranked higher than any duelists in our division. The captain of their team, Marz, could copy any fighting style. The other two duelists were twin girls, Leik and Lye, who could shape-shift. Daimon was assigned to Marz, and Blaze and Resno would fight the twins.

My thoughts returned to the reality that I might be forced to murder people. I hated myself, but I rationalized that if I obeyed Kallisto, Taurik would live.

Once spectators started arriving, Daimon ushered the team into the dressing room. “This is a big match, but I know we can beat these guys!” He examined our faces, looking from one of us to the next. “I have a surprise.” He paused to let anticipation electrify the atmosphere. “Some *very* special guests are going to be at today’s match!”

“Who?” the team chorused.

“I can’t say.”

Valisa, Blaze, and Melee scrambled to lean out the

dressing room door, trying to get a peek at the surprise guests.

"Ladies, you'll have plenty of time to survey the crowd before the match starts."

Blaze and Melee instantly straightened, but Valisa continued to peer from the doorway. "No matter who it is, we must act professional because we represent Abervania." He assessed our expressions. "Are we ready to beat Vainbalt?"

"*Yes*!"

"Hands in! Duel it on three! One, two, three!"

"*Duel it*!"

Then, without wasting a second, everyone except for Daimon and me rushed onto the field. I couldn't even look because I didn't want to see those giddy faces I might have to kill.

Studying my expression, Daimon frowned. "Are you okay?"

I almost lost control and started crying, but now was not the time for weakness. "Yeah. I'm just—putting off the surprise as long as possible." I forced a smile, and he nodded. I was relieved that he bought it, but part of me wished he hadn't.

"So you're ready for the masses?"

"Sure."

It seemed like an hour elapsed by the time we walked through the tunnel to the Grobe and onto the field. My heart raced. I was terrified to see the important guests.

I tried not to look into the stands, but within seconds, I spotted the visitors. My heart sank. They were smiling and applauding with everyone, their expressions eager. They seemed so normal. I made eye contact with the beautiful woman, and we stared at each other.

She had flawless, white skin, and her platinum hair was as pure as it would have been on a newborn baby. Her mate was attractive, too, but I had seen him many times. He and his brother had been the subject of many History of Aspasia lessons.

Daimon and I reached the bench, and I took my place as benchwarmer.

As Daimon gave everyone last-minute pointers, Valisa whispered to Melee, “I can’t believe Deo and Rhaine Clevist are here.”

Both teams took their places on the field. “Duelers at the ready!” the commentator barked. All duelists crouched, prepared for their opponents. Marz was tanned, red-headed, and short but built like a brick wall. The twins were tanned, brunette, and petite but limber.

“Duel it on three! “One, two—” Electricity filled the air. “Three!”

The duelists lunged at one another, but I couldn’t stop wondering about the Clevists. *What could they have done to turn Kallisto against them?* One of the twins fell to the ground, and there was a flurry of activity in Daimon’s sector, but I couldn’t focus on the duels.

“It didn’t take Resno long to beat Lye!” Meena was gleeful.

“No.”

“Vainbalt is ranked high, too!”

“Yeah.” My voice betrayed my disinterest.

Meena stared at me. "Are you okay?"

"Yeah. I'm just concentrating on the match."

"Are you sure?"

"Yeah. I, uh, I just have a lot going on." I smiled, but her frown lingered.

Without thinking, I glanced at Deo and Rhaine who were engrossed in the match. Deo's gingerbread hair was just as I remembered from Professor Yttira's visions in History of Aspasia, and Rhaine's alabaster skin and high cheek bones reminded me of Queen Elizabeth I. Like mine, her hair was so blonde that it was almost white. She and Deo looked so relaxed and carefree. *But how could I live without Taurik if Kallisto killed him?*

When the match ended, I wasn't sure how long it had lasted. Only when everyone on our bench ran onto the field and cheered with the team while the crowd roared its approval did I realize we'd won. The atmosphere was electrified, but it seemed separate from me. Experiencing everything from the sidelines made me feel not like a spectator but like an outsider.

I willed myself to get up from the bench, but I remained where I was. Depression sank in as I perceived the type of person I was about to become. I had to love Taurik. Why else would I give up my morals?

I started. Meena was staring at me from the field, frowning. Attempting to act as if everything was normal, I pasted on a perfect smile and hurried onto the field to join my teammates in celebration. I embraced each teammate—even Resno with whom I'd never had an intimate conversation. When I made eye contact with Meena, she grinned but a trace of suspicion still lingered in her eyes.

"We'll talk after we leave," she whispered.

I wish. "I can't. I'm going—somewhere."

Her brow furrowed. "Where?"

"A new place with the headmistress." *Was that safe to say?*

"Really?"

"Yes," I lied. "I think she's introducing me to another trainer."

"But I thought *she* was your trainer."

"No. It—it didn't work with her schedule."

"But I thought—"

"Loddy, are you ready?" Kallisto had appeared soundlessly. Her eyes lacked emotion.

"Yes."

Kallisto smiled and nodded at Meena.

Her voice guarded, Meena said, "Headmistress."

I smiled half-heartedly. "See you later." But I didn't know when I'd see Meena again.

"See you," she said reluctantly.

"Loddy!" Daimon yelled, "Where are you going? We're celebrating our victory!"

"She has a meeting," Kallisto snapped. "Goodbye!"

"See you later, Loddy!"

"Okay!" I forced a smile, wishing I could have celebrated like everyone else.

Once out of the Grobe, Kallisto extended her hand. When I hesitated, she hissed, "Take it!" I grabbed her hand and almost shrank from her icy touch. Within seconds, we were transported to a spacious parlor in a grand mansion that, unlike Kallisto's office building, was made entirely of wood.

The parlor replicated the stiff, cold atmosphere of Kallisto's office, featuring a couch that was upholstered in the same fiery red. No paintings occupied the walls, but multiple loo tables showcasing various statuettes were positioned around the room. Vintage books packed shelves that lined every wall. At the far end of the room, a wide spiral staircase led to an unseen floor. As I looked closer, I saw that a thin layer of dust covered the books.

I was puzzled as to why Kallisto, a fire manipulator, would live in a house made of wood. It seemed a curious and unnecessary hazard.

Kallisto grabbed me, forcing me to face her. "If Deo asks, you're from an outer crozii called Delutz. Are we clear?"

"Yes."

"If you even hesitate to obey me, Taurik dies. Understood?" Her eyes were manic.

"Yes." My jaw set.

She searched my eyes and her nails dug into my shoulders. "If you fail, everything is ruined. You won't escape me—*I promise*."

I nodded, refusing to show the despair I felt. *There has to be a way out of this—but how?*

At that point, Kesta entered the room wearing a sparkling white evening gown. "Hello, all." She and I made eye contact, and I thought I detected shame in hers.

Kallisto let go of me. "Kesta, I'm going to change. Keep an eye on Loddy. The distinguished guests should be arriving soon."

"Of course."

As Kallisto ascended the wooden staircase, a weight was lifted from the room. Everyone breathed more easily. I tried to look at Kesta, but she dodged my gaze. I decided to break the silence. "This house isn't what I thought it would be."

"Not big enough?" She forced nonchalance.

"Oh, it fits her gargantuan ego all right. What I meant was the wood." I walked around ostensibly examining the details of the carved woodwork without seeing them.

"What's wrong with the wood?"

"Don't you think it's impractical for a fire manipulator to own a wooden home?"

Kesta frowned, like she was contemplating some secret around and around in her head. "She's—unpredictable."

"Maybe so." *Now the hard part.* "Kesta, why are you doing this?"

She looked at me for a moment before quickly averting her eyes. "I'm in too deep." "You're hiding something, aren't you?"

She paused and then nodded.

I wasn't angry. She, too, was a pawn in Kallisto's game. "I know you can't tell me the secret. I just hope you can find the courage to stand up to her one day."

We made eye contact until we were interrupted by a tall, beautiful woman wearing an off-the-shoulder, side-slit gown that exposed toned arms and legs. Despite her build, the woman didn't look human. Her grey skin glimmered along with her sparkling black gown in the incandescent light.

"Kesta, they're here." Her voice was low, almost like a man's. When she saw me, her eyes rested on mine. Their sclera was black instead of white, and her irises were crimson. *Did I imagine it, or was she reluctant to look away?*

"They are?" Kesta asked, her voice anxious. "Well, let them in!"

"No need." A familiar voice reverberated through the hallway. The two most powerful people in Aspasia strolled into the room where they would lose their lives because of me.

21

IDENTITY

Kesta and the strange woman bowed to Deo and Rhaine, and I followed. "You don't have to bow," Deo said, a smile in his voice.

Rhaine carried herself with perfect grace, flowing like a gentle stream. When her cream-colored irises found mine, she lost interest in the others in the room. She came and sat next to me, gleaming from the aura radiating about her. Somehow, she seemed familiar.

"Are you Loddy?" she asked, her voice a soft soprano.

"Yes, Queen Rhaine." I was so nervous that my voice almost cracked.

"I've heard so much about you," she said, smiling.

I couldn't believe she knew who I was. "*You've* heard about *me*?"

"Of course she has!" Deo boomed, joining us. He wasn't as polished as his wife, but his confidence confirmed that he was used to commanding a room. However, when our eyes met, his smile faltered, as if he was seeing something in my eyes he had been seeking for a long time.

Observing his gaze, the Queen chided, "Staring

isn't polite." Her playful tone held a hint of suspicion. "Deo?"

"Yes?" Deo said, still peering at me.

"It isn't polite to stare."

"I wasn't staring." He shifted his gaze to Rhaine. "She just reminded me of—"

"—of someone you used to know?" The voice came from the top of the staircase. Kallisto had overheard Deo. Her smirk hinted at dark satisfaction as, clad in a sleek black gown that displayed her toned biceps, she descended to the foyer.

"And here is our gracious host." Deo beamed as Kallisto bowed slightly to the royals.

"Your Majesties."

"No need for that." Deo winked.

"Only paying my respects." Derision laced her voice.

"You've been a good friend for a long time, so you're like family."

"Whatever you say, Deo." They embraced, and I felt sick.

"Rhaine, it's so nice to see you." Kallisto and Rhaine hugged. "Thank you for attending the duel. I know the students enjoy seeing both of you every year."

Rhaine beamed. "We love seeing the students, too—and we take pleasure in escaping our royal duties."

"I know you're hungry after your trying day. I've asked my chefs to prepare your favorites—Pampolonian steak for Deo and lyvites for you."

Deo's smile became even broader at the mention of

Pampolonian steak. "Kallisto, you've outdone yourself, as usual."

At dinner, I sat between King Deo, who was seated at the head of the table, and Kallisto, who was seated on my right. The Queen and Kesta sat across from us. The odd woman had disappeared.

As we ate our shrimp cocktail appetizers, Deo turned to me. "Loddy, I understand you're from Delutz?"

"Yes."

"That's odd. I'd heard from more than one reliable source that you were from Earth."

My jaw dropped. Beside me, I felt Kallisto tense. I only made eye contact with Deo. "I assure you those rumors are false, Your Majesty."

"So you expect me to believe *you* over my advisers?" He feigned innocence but his voice was tinged with suspicion.

As the guests held their breath in anticipation, I knew I had to stick to my story. "Yes," I said, forcing myself to sound confident. I fixed him with unfaltering eyes.

When he started laughing, the room exhaled in relief. "Kallisto, you were right about her. She *is* smart." He centered in on me. "I wouldn't trust my advisers, either. That's why I don't most of the time."

I laughed and breathed easier. I feared I might have botched Kallisto's operation before it started.

"Kallisto has been keeping you under wraps for a while. She told me you unlocked all ten conversion stones?"

"Yes, sir."

He stared at me. "That would mean that you are the most powerful student Abervania has ever had."

"That is what they tell me, sir." I didn't want to sound cocky.

"Which would mean—" he made eye contact with me "—that *you* are more powerful than *I*."

I fidgeted. "That would be a matter of opinion."

"No, it would not."

I suspected that I should have felt uncomfortable with the most powerful Aspasian telling me I could overpower him, but I didn't.

His voice still enthusiastic, he continued, "*I* only unlocked one conversion stone. Did you know that?"

"No."

"My wife and every other god unlocked only one." He paused from taking a bite to stare at me, just as the Queen had, as if I was the only other person in the room. "Of course, this isn't the first time a student has unlocked more than one conversion stone, but never has one unlocked all ten. Do you realize what this means?"

I decided to play dumb. "No."

"This means that *you* are the most powerful being in all of Aspasia, in all of existence—second only to God Himself."

I didn't feel powerful. Kallisto was the powerful one. She controlled my every move.

"You may appear modest, but your abilities can't be taken lightly. That's why Rhaine and I are here."

My heart started pounding.

"Would you be interested in living with us while being tutored by the greatest Aspasian instructors? These would include Rhaine, the other gods, and myself. We'd guide you in becoming the leader Aspasia needs, and it is hoped that we'd learn from you, too."

I couldn't believe what I was hearing. They actually wanted me to live with them! "I—I don't know what to say."

The Queen spoke up quickly. "Of course, you don't have to make a decision now." Her eyes were warm and comforting.

I wanted to squeal. They were offering to swoop me away from Kallisto's toxicity. Of course, Taurik would have to come with me. To live with a real king and queen would be like living a fairy tale. Unfortunately, my life would never be a fairy tale as long as I was Kallisto's slave. "I'll consider it." I forced a smile.

"That's all we ask, as long as you consider with haste," Deo said, smiling.

"Deo!" Rhaine glared at him before shifting her attention to me. "Take as long as you wish."

"How nice," Kallisto almost spat. That Deo and Rhaine Clevist had offered me—the thorn in Kallisto's side—the perfect life, was killing her. "Sadly, Loddy won't be able to accept."

Hope and positivity disappeared as the atmosphere tensed. This was it—the eleventh hour. The time had come for me to do the unthinkable to the people who had just promised me the Aspasian galaxy.

"What do you mean *she can't accept*?" Deo's voice remained polite but held traces of anger. "You told me she would accept if she chose."

Kallisto stood. "She can't accept because *you* won't have the power to provide tutelage for her."

Deo rose from his chair, towering over her. "What do you mean? Are you threatening me?"

I hadn't noticed the hunched woman appear in the doorway behind us, or the alien woman in the shabby robe in the doorway on the opposite side of the room.

The old woman's face and hands were wrinkled and grey-tinged, like the alien's. Her nails were unnaturally long, and, since they were unpainted, the cracks running through them were visible. Her eyes were pale green. She inched closer, but the alien woman stayed where she was.

Deo and Rhaine noted their presence.

Kallisto ignored the new guests. She looked amused as she continued, "'Threaten' has such negative implications. But seeing as I plan to remove you from office, then, yes, I'm threatening you. You see, my plan has been in motion for many years. You'll never stop me now."

Deo looked incredulous. "What are you talking about? Aspasia is a constitutional monarchy! Only those within the ruling families can fill the highest positions of power."

"Not for long," Kallisto almost sang. "But don't worry about the details, Deo. I have everything taken care of."

Rhaine stood, her eyes blazing. "You're talking madness, Kallisto. What's wrong with you?"

"Nothing is wrong with me. You and Deo and all your followers have been running this galaxy into the ground for far too long. You've waged unnecessary war when you should have been paying attention to major problems. Who knows how much you've cost everyone financially, or how many innocent lives have been taken because of your and Alexander's argument concerning how justified you were in murdering his son? Beyond that, you bar all but your inner circle from occupying seats of power that could be filled by some of the greatest, non-royal minds this universe has to offer."

"It's a *monarchy!*" Deo raged.

"If the positions are only reserved for the royal families, shouldn't the king's own brother have been admitted to the inner circle?"

Realization dawned on Deo. "So *that's* what this is about."

Flames darted in Kallisto's eyes. "That's what this has *always* been about!"

Kallisto's reasoning began to make sense to me. The gods had stripped Deo's brother, Prodrian, of all power because they believed him to be power-hungry and evil. Now, Kallisto wanted to avenge Prodrian by ousting all the gods.

Deo spoke quietly. "He was too dangerous to be in a position of power."

"He wasn't!" The flames in her eyes became more pronounced. "His ideas would have made Aspasia better than it is now!"

"If we had implemented his ideas, Aspasia wouldn't even be here. How can you justify what he did to those phoenix-holders to create that monster?"

"He did what had to be done!"

"He had everything he needed but he still wanted more."

Kallisto gripped her chair. "He wanted to protect Aspasia no matter who or what opposed us. No one would have complained once he was able to protect us from every possible threat."

"No one should have that much power, Kallisto!" Deo struggled to control his impatience. "That's why we've separated our branches of government among ten people instead of placing any one branch in one person's hands. Checks and balances must be in place, or what happened to Prodrian could occur again."

Kesta's eyes rested on Deo. She felt ashamed because she didn't want to oppose him, but like me, she was trapped.

"We shall see." Kallisto turned to the old woman. "Mab, you know what to do."

As Mab hobbled toward me, Rhaine clutched Deo for protection. I avoided their gazes.

"Kallisto, I *demand* that you stop this now!" Deo's voice quavered as if this was the first time he had never been in control.

The old woman placed her hands on my arms, closed her eyes and chanted in an unknown language under her breath. "*Sheek sheek ow sheek sheek ow! Kappah lappah vichy*!"

I looked at Kallisto. "What is she doing to me?"

"Don't worry. She's preparing you to slaughter these people for the dictators they are." Her eyes sparkled as she watched Deo and Rhaine, happy to envision their deaths at last.

Rhaine dropped Deo's arm as Kallisto's plan dawned on her. "You're going to make the *child* murder us?"

"Of course. With all her power, the massacre will be over in seconds." She and Deo made eye contact.

"I'm done!" Deo yelled. "Crastimus! Theon! We're leaving!" He started out with Rhaine, but the alien woman blocked the doorway.

"They can't hear you, Deo," Kallisto said with sheer pleasure in her voice. "Only the people in this room can hear you now. I've made sure my friends are in the right places even if that means being in your guard. No one is coming to save you."

Deo stiffened, his body quaking with anger. Rhaine looked fearful, and that sickened me. I was about to murder them, and seeing the hope leave her made everything worse.

"*You vile dragon*!" Deo yelled, "I never thought you of all people would turn on me."

"Surprise." Kallisto's sneer was chilling.

"I just ask that you spare my wife. Let her go, and do what you will with me."

Kallisto sauntered toward them, contemplating his request. She stood before Rhaine and looked her straight in the eye. "You're both dead to me."

Rhaine stared back at her, as Deo raised his arm. "Do not strike her, Deo. She's not worth it."

Kallisto's laugh was mirthless. "How admirable. The Queen stays classy to the very end. Too bad no one will know it."

I felt a strange sensation develop in my core that spread throughout my body. It was as if I was being cleared of something that I didn't know was there. I began to feel open and unhindered like my body could do anything. *Oh, no.* I wondered if Mab was undoing whatever had prevented the full extent of my powers.

Did that mean that I would not have control, but that someone else would? *Were they assuring that Deo and Rhaine would be murdered even if I backed out?*

"This is where I leave you, Deo. Good riddance," Kallisto said. "Kesta?"

"Yes?" Kesta looked helpless.

"The time has finally come to watch our beloved King and Queen die the deaths they deserve—from a reasonable distance, of course."

"Of course," Kesta almost whispered. She seemed so frail and disgraced at the realization of the person she had become.

Kallisto faced me for the first time since we had entered the dining room. "Don't disappoint me." She turned to the others. "Mab and Rae, come."

Mab and Rae followed her to the door at the end of the room. Kallisto turned. "Oh, and don't even think about looking for an exit. The doors in this house are specially reinforced such that only those of whom I approve may pass through them." She surveyed the room one last time as if observing her own artwork. "Farewell."

"Don't be so sure about that, Kallisto." It was the voice I'd been yearning to hear for days.

22

Reunion

Taurik stood in the doorway, his expression triumphant. With him was a person I thought I'd never see again.

Although Professor Omega had been robust, his skin now hung loosely from his body. "Omega?" Deo sounded pleasantly surprised. "Is that you?"

"Yes, Your Majesty." Omega bowed, and Taurik followed suit. "Though I look thinner than the last time we met. They don't feed the prisoners well here."

"*Prisoners*? Do you mean to tell me that *Kallisto* has done this to you?"

Indicating Taurik, the professor said, "To me *and* to this young student."

"Kallisto, is this true?"

Kallisto's body had become rigid, and her face conveyed pure hatred toward everyone in the room. She spoke through gritted teeth. "*Why are you here*?" Flames appeared in her hands."I'm here to tell Loddy who she really is."

"So it *is* true," Professor Omega whispered.

"Who is she?" Deo asked, his voice barely audible. He and Rhaine clutched hands, peering at me with a sense of recognition.

"Taurik, I swear, I'll—"

"Kill me?" He laughed. "The secret will do that anyway! Face it, Kallisto, you've lost! And once I'm gone, you won't have any leverage over Loddy. She'll be able to live the life she was meant for."

Did he mean to sacrifice himself for me? I was frightened. "Taurik, what do you mean?"

The professor, King, and Queen gazed at me, seeing the truth before it was spoken. *How could they see what I couldn't?*

Kallisto furrowed her brow. "Don't do it!"

Taurik reached out to me. "Loddy—"

"Taurik, don't do this. I don't want you to die." Tears formed around our eyes. It was the first time I'd ever seen him cry. His tears were so clear.

"Your real name is—"

"Lodesyia!"

The voice sounded familiar, but it couldn't be!

As if in a dream, Zander burst into the room followed by Malicious, Cash, and the beloved people who had raised me, Uncle William and Aunt Maggie. Their warm smiles conveyed the unconditional love that had never left them since I'd disappeared.

Aunt Maggie's baby blue eyes brimmed with tears. "Loddy."

"Hey, Sweetie," Uncle William chimed in. He was wearing the cowboy hat I'd seen him don many days in the field to keep the sun at bay.

"I'm so glad to see all of you—but you can't be here! It's too dangerous!" I realized that if the dark phoenix emerged, everyone around me could die.

"I tried to tell them, but they wouldn't listen." Malicious rolled her eyes.

Deo observed Zander with wonder. "You're Alexander's son, aren't you?"

Zander had to have been the lost prince the students had discussed in History of Aspasia. Rhaine's voice quivered. "Did—did you say—?"

"Lodesyia? Yes." Zander pointed to me. "Loddy is your daughter, Your Majesties."

Deo and Rhaine gazed at me, their eyes filled with tears.

But how could I be Princess Lodesyia? I had a dark phoenix inside me. Kallisto had told me the phoenix had entered my body after it found me in an orphanage. Then I remembered the unknown blob we had discussed in Professor Yttira's class, the one who had taken the princess. I whipped around to face Kallisto. "You did it! *You* kidnapped me!"

A cold smile formed across Kallisto's lips.

His voice filled with rage, Deo asked, "Well, did you?"

She avoided his gaze and only stared at me.

"Answer me!" Deo strode toward her.

Still staring at me, Kallisto said, "Yes. *I* kidnapped your daughter."

I was appalled. "You want me to murder *my own parents*?"

Deo moved to smack Kallisto.

"Deo, do *not* strike her." Rhaine's voice was firm.

"Give me one reason why I shouldn't smash this

viper's face in!" He glared at Kallisto who looked bemused.

"Because—"

"Because it isn't *worth* it? Rhaine, you know how many sleepless nights we've had, how long it has taken us to finally accept that she isn't coming back." He clenched his fists.

"If that's the logic that you'll be able to accept tomorrow, then do what you want now."

Slowly, he unclenched his fists, but he didn't take his eyes from Kallisto.

Aunt Maggie and Taurik were both looking at me, and neither of them seemed frightened. Their gazes conveyed their belief that we were going to survive. Zander's and my eyes met. I couldn't believe he was alive. It seemed I had been in the process of letting him go forever, and here he was.

Then Kallisto started laughing.

"Why do you snicker, witch?" Deo asked.

She peered into his eyes with unwavering strength. "Because this—changes—nothing."

"What are you talking about? When we get out of here—"

"*When* you get out of here?" She sneered. "You'll never place a foot outside this house. And neither will anyone else—besides the princess and me."

"I don't know if you've realized it," Deo said, "but you're outnumbered."

Kallisto's grin widened. "Don't be so sure."

"You're truly disillusioned if you think you're

going to beat all of us."

"You forget that I have the most powerful being at my disposal." She smiled at me.

"Lodesyia doesn't want anything to do with you."

"Lodesyia doesn't have a choice."

My thoughts turned to the old woman. "What did Mab do?"

"You'll soon find out."

Deo spun Kallisto around by her wrist. "Of what do you speak?"

"Everyone will be disappointed when they hear that the princess, after uncovering her true identity, exploded in rage because she was too distraught to handle the truth. In doing so, she unleashed the dark phoenix who burnt down her poor headmistress's home—killing her parents, the king and queen."

At the mention of the dark phoenix, Deo paled.

Evily's assessment had been correct. Kallisto was planning to unleash the dark phoenix.

"Afterwards, everyone will pity the princess, but they will view her with suspicion. They'll say she can't possibly become queen in her current state, so a regent will be appointed in her place. And who should the galaxy look to besides she who found the lost princess and took her under her wing? It doesn't hurt that said woman has all the right friends in the Aspasian government. So my appointment shouldn't be met with significant opposition."

"Ow! You burned me!" Deo yelled, dropping Kallisto's arm and cradling his hand.

"Face it." Kallisto spat. "I've already won."

"It all makes sense now. You hid the phoenix inside Lodesyia all these years."

I started to cry. "Why would I do anything for you, Kallisto, after all my reasons for living are dead?"

Without looking at me, she said, "I'm done talking to you. Now, if you'll excuse me, I have somewhere to be."

"I'm not letting you leave!" Deo grabbed for her, but his hand passed through her fading arm. "What is this witchcraft?"

"Taurik is fading, too!" Malicious yelled.

Sure enough, Taurik's body was disappearing just as Kallisto's was.

"Taurik! No!" I lunged for him, but I couldn't grab hold. *She really was going to control me after they were dead.*

"Keep fighting," Taurik said, his waning voice desperate.

"I told you, Deo," Kallisto called. "I've already won. Have a wonderful family reunion." Then she and Taurik were gone.

I could feel everyone staring at me, wondering what was about to happen.

Rhaine touched my arm. "Lodesyia, sweetie." I looked into her eyes which were concerned but, like Taurik and Aunt Maggie's, filled with strength.

"She took Taurik." My voice shook. "I'm frightened."

"I know." Her voice was comforting.

"I don't want to kill anyone."

Her voice was kind but firm. "Lodesyia, you can

change this. You don't have to give in to the dark phoenix."

"I'm not strong enough. I've practiced, but she has made the phoenix invincible now."

"You're invincible, too." Aunt Maggie squeezed my hand.

"Ya can do whatever ya set yer mind to, Loddy or Lodesyia, or whatever yer name is." Uncle William had the same twinkle in his eye that I'd missed.

If I let the dark phoenix take over, my world would continue to be on Kallisto's terms. My only wish would be to see Taurik, and Kallisto hadn't promised that she would let me.

"Hey." Zander was still tanned, but his eyes were bright red instead of dark brown since he was no longer on Earth. "I know you can beat this."

"How do you know?"

"Because—"

Debilitating pain struck my gut, and I keeled over. I grasped my stomach in an attempt to stop the agony, but I couldn't. "It's happening!"

"Everyone get back!" Deo yelled.

"*No*!" The pain was so intense that I couldn't lift my head, and my vision began to fade.

Rhaine's voice was filled with fear. "Deo, is there *anything* we can do?"

"I'm willin' to do whatever helps." Aunt Maggie couldn't stop staring at me.

Malicious, speaking for her and Cash, said, "We are, too."

"We can't do anything." Deo sounded hopeless.

"The phoenix is more powerful than all of us."

"Surely—" Rhaine began.

But I could no longer hear or see what was going on around me. I was losing control. I tried to yell, but no sound issued from my lips. I wanted to scream at the dark phoenix to leave my loved ones alone. I wanted to reclaim my identity as Princess Lodesyia, but hope was running out.

No! I *must* fight! I focused on clearing my head, and as I did, I could feel the dark phoenix's spirit move throughout my body like blood surging through my veins. *What had Mab done to grant the phoenix this much freedom?* Then my head cleared.

Well, well, well. Little Lodesyia has finally taken control. Too bad it won't last.

"Oh, but it will." I hoped my voice sounded resolute.

No, your control won't last because even though Mab's spell unlocked the full extent of your powers—the ones to which I'm more accustomed, it takes a certain knowledge to navigate all of the powers at once.

"But we both have access to those powers."

True. But you won't overpower me. Before, the spell pre-empted my ability to take over whenever I wanted, but now I can take over when I wish.

"What if I'm more strong-willed than you think?"

The phoenix doubled over with the breathy laughter of a smoker. *Your mind is nothing compared with mine. You would need years of practice to combat even a small percentage of what I'm about to throw at you.*

Confidence reigned foremost in my voice. "We'll see."

Yes, we will see. But before I destroy your life, let me say that inhabiting your body was the best thing I ever did. I couldn't have picked anyone with more to lose. You have everything anyone could ever want: fame, power, love. Now, I'm going to warp all of it so that you'll never have any hope of living the good life again.

Face it. Your claim to the life of Princess Lodesyia is over. But with as much power as you have, you'd be crazy to think you wouldn't have a test like me. Because that's the cost of power: being willing to pay the highest price to gain it and once it's yours, to keep it. And with power like yours, you must pay the supreme price—the identity that wields it.

And now, I'm going to kill you—but not in the sense of destroying your body. No. I will kill your soul so that all you are is a walking body, an empty shell, useless except to do Kallisto's bidding. Goodbye, Loddy.

I lost my hold on reality as my soul ejected from my body like debris shot out of a volcano. Then, as if standing a few feet away, I watched my body.

The phoenix was me. My face appeared older and menacing. My hands had morphed into claws because the phoenix wasn't accustomed to the mechanism of human hands. My eyes took me by surprise. They were a disturbing dark violet that hinted that the body's inhabitant was cold and heartless.

Deo and Rhaine hunched together, as did Malicious,

Cash, Uncle William, and Aunt Maggie. Professor Omega and Zander gazed at my body, waiting for the phoenix to make a move.

"Well?" the phoenix spat. "What are you going to do now, all-powerful Deo?"

Deo stared it straight in the eye. "My daughter won't let you win."

The dark phoenix examined my body over which it now had full control. "I don't know if you realize it, but your daughter—is *gone*. And she won't be back until you're dead."

"No!" Zander took a step toward the phoenix. "She'll beat you. Even if it's not today, she'll defeat you, Filth!"

The dark phoenix looked at Zander as if seeing him for the first time. "You aren't supposed to be alive."

"It's funny how things happen, isn't it?"

"How did you survive?" Behind the layers of contempt and forced indifference, real curiosity peaked in the phoenix's voice.

"Wouldn't *you* like to know." Zander's voice was gleeful.

"*Tell me*!"

Zander grinned. "You couldn't even destroy me."

The phoenix spoke through clenched teeth. "What are you talking about?"

"You mangled my body, but you didn't destroy my spirit. You could have if you hadn't absorbed me so fast after attacking my body, but you couldn't wait."

"*You lie!*"

"It's true. Here I am. When you absorbed my phoenix-spirit, you also absorbed my soul—but you didn't get all of it. The rest of my soul was still inside my body, even though it seemed like I was dead.

"As you know, a phoenix's body can rejuvenate with time. I was living inside Loddy, so I began to rejuvenate inside her."

So that's why he had been able to mentally communicate with me. He and I had shared the same body, the same mind.

"My incomplete entranx pattern was able to repair itself since I was present in two different bodies. Had my entire soul been inside just my dead body, my entranx pattern would not have been able to function. To repair itself, my entranx pattern needed the live body that Loddy provided. Once I was healed, my soul and body merged."

"Aren't we smart?" The phoenix's tone dripped with disgust.

"See, Loddy?" Zander yelled, "The phoenix is *not* all-powerful! You *can* beat it!"

Zander's story gave me hope. Zander had been less than an entire soul, but he fought for his identity until he finally won. I could feel strength radiating throughout my limbs and mind.

"You were always so theatrical, Prince Alexander." The phoenix's air of caution suggested that his failure to kill Zander had shaken him, but he acted tough. "I'm done talking!"

The atmosphere of the room tensed. Rhaine and Aunt Maggie looked terrified, which inspired me to act. I began clearing my head by thinking of all the reasons I had to defeat the phoenix. To commandeer such power, I'd have to pass the test for the identity that wielded that power.

As I reached deep inside for a secret reserve of strength, I began to appreciate the blessing of free choice. Free choice was indeed a precious gift from God, one that I had taken for granted. My mind cleared, and, as Princess Lodesyia, I observed my surroundings. The mansion started to crumble where the phoenix had shot fire while I was concentrating. The group huddled together.

What are you doing? The phoenix's voice sounded at once disgusted and surprised.

"I'm taking control of what's mine."

This life isn't yours anymore. Get out!

The phoenix tried pushing me out again, but I braced against it. It was like pushing opposite a steel wall in my mind. "I'm not going anywhere! This is my body, my family, my life! You can't have it!"

Let's see how strong you are after I kill one of your friends.

My body sauntered toward Rhaine who was huddled against Deo.

Let me show you what an onslaught of ice shards can do to a person's body.

My hands extended involuntarily. "No! Stop!" My soul could not bear to watch my body harm anyone, let alone Rhaine.

Rhaine and Deo huddled tighter.

The phoenix spoke through my voice. "Goodbye,

Queen Rhaine."

"Whatever ya are, ya'd better git outta Loddy this instant!" yelled Uncle William.

"I will take care of *you* soon enough."

"No ya won't! Loddy'll come back before ya even get the chance. You're nothin' but a weak li'l namby-pamby."

"I've heard enough from you, Grandpa."

"I'm talkin' to ya, and ya'd better listen to me! Yer weak! Weak, I tell ya! You don't deserve to occupy the same body as my Loddy!"

I felt the anger intensify in the phoenix.

"He's right," I said, provoking the anger. "You are weak. You couldn't even break Mab's lousy spell."

Shut up! That spell was one of the most powerful in existence!

"It wasn't *that* powerful. You're just making excuses."

I see what you're doing. You're trying to anger me so that you can take advantage of my weakness. Too bad it's not going to work. "Goodbye, Queen Rhaine!"

Ice rushed through my veins. I struggled to gain control but failed. This was it. My parents were going to die, and I would never share another touching moment with them.

But before the first shard flew from my hand, a new presence inhabited my mind, commanding me to stop the ice.

"Zander, how—?"

"No time to explain." His voice in my mind raced.

"Focus on inhabiting every part of your body that you can."

"Okay." I concentrated and I was able to take control more easily.

What are you doing, Alexander? Don't you know when to quit?

I was having trouble telling the phoenix and Zander apart. They felt like the same entity.

You have to stop! Now!

I pushed my awareness through my hands and feet, my torso, neck, and finally my face. Within moments, I fully commanded my body again.

The group was glancing between me and something beside me. I looked and saw Zander, whose eyes were closed as he focused on keeping the phoenix at bay. *How was he in my mind?* I made eye contact with Aunt Maggie. "It's me."

"Loddy?"

"Yes, but I'm not sure how this is happening."

Deo joined the conversation. He sounded confused. "We aren't sure what's happening, either. Can you communicate with Zander?"

"No. I think he's merged with the phoenix."

"Merged?" Rhaine asked, alarmed, "Deo, how is this possible?"

"I have a theory."

"What is it? Hurry!" I was on edge because the phoenix could take control any second.

"Zander could have reunited with the segment of his phoenix-spirit that the dark phoenix stole after it tried to kill him."

"I thought Zander's phoenix-spirit merged with Zander's soul when Zander returned to his body."

"That's the funny thing about phoenix-spirits," he said. "They can function without souls. In fact, soul and phoenix-spirit are separate until late in the phoenix-controller's life when the soul and spirit have been together so long that they merge completely. But since Zander is still young, his soul had only partially merged with the phoenix-spirit before it was ripped from his body."

I could feel two forces attacking one another inside me, but I didn't react. I was afraid if I did, Zander would lose focus.

"A trace of his soul to which his mind was still attuned must have been on his phoenix-spirit inside the dark phoenix allowing him to flit between his body and your mind at any time."

So Zander had access to my thoughts about Taurik. Great. "What am I supposed to do? Just wait?"

"I guess," Deo said, unsure. "Zander is probably trying to weaken the phoenix long enough for you to rescue us. Can you move?"

"Yes." Part of thc mansion was still burning. I had to act before the fire spread. "Didn't Kallisto say the house was reinforced by a spell?"

"Yeah, but you can perform magic." Cash spoke as if this information should have been apparent to everyone. "You can do anything."

"I've never practiced magic." *Evily would have known the right spell to use. If only I could teleport her into the mansion. Wait.* "If I can do anything, I have access to transport entranx, right?"

"Of course!" Enthusiasm spread through the room.

"So I could teleport everyone out of here?"

"Do it, Lodesyia!" Deo was on edge, "Zander can't hold that thing off much longer."

I closed my eyes and cleared my head. I envisioned transporting everyone. I made their transport my sole desire. In my mind's eye, as if in space, I could see the full scope of my powers in a wide array of psychedelic colors. I saw recognizable hues as well as those that didn't exist in reality, both of which reminded me of my entranx pattern.

With my eyes still closed, I focused on my entranx pattern. A bright violet orb materialized and began hurtling toward me. The orb entered my body and was at my disposal.

When I opened my eyes, everyone was staring at me. "Well?" Deo asked.

"I'm ready. Huddle!"

Once everyone clustered around me, I closed my eyes. The new energy surged throughout my body like electricity, as eager for me to release it as a thoroughbred at the starting gate. I thought about where I wanted us to go, then tapped the power lightly.

23

PRINCESS

I felt a slight brush of air before opening my eyes. Chaste Palez. Surrounding me were all my friends, cheering. I started to cry.

Aunt Maggie embraced me. "I'm so proud of you."

"Me, too," Rhaine said, joining our hugging session.

Warmly Professor Omega added, "We're all proud of you, Princess."

"Th—thank you." I had saved my entire world, so I wouldn't have to battle Kallisto alone. I had my family and friends to help me.

"Where are we?" Uncle William asked, observing the marble columns.

"Chaste Palez," said a soft voice.

"Meda?" Deo asked, confused. "What are you doing here?"

"I'm here to lock the dark phoenix away—again." Meda was pale and sported a brown pixie cut. She turned to me. "Loddy, you may tell Zander to let go. I'll take care of everything."

"Okay." I closed my eyes. *You can let go now, Zander. Meda is here.*

Thank goodness. Zander sounded relieved.

Zander retreated, and instantly I felt a new force, Meda, attack the phoenix.

Meda had closed her eyes. I assumed separating the phoenix completely from my mind was impossible because it was a part of my soul. She chanted a spell under her breath to again bind the dark phoenix to my mind. "There! That should do it."

Upon seeing that Zander was once again in control of his body, Deo patted Zander's back and the crowd cheered for him. "You saved our lives, Alexander," Deo said, "I'm eternally grateful."

"All I ask is that you speak to my father."

A crooked smile formed on Deo's lips. "Deal." He caught Meda's eyes. "Meda, where have you been?" He sounded frustrated and elated at the same time. "Did you catch Kallisto?"

"Kallisto has fled to an unknown crozii. It's unlikely that we'll ever find her, but we're trying. One of my aides saw her flee with an alternator and another student. Their names are Calix and Carrigan."

Oh, no. Taurik was right. Calix and Carrigan had been spying on me.

"Excuse me." My heart pounded. "Calix and Carrigan. What did you call one of them?"

"An alternator—one who shares an existence with another person, but neither can inhabit reality at the same time."

Carrigan had been the alternator, and his partner was Cannon. That's what Cannon had tried telling me, and that's why I heard both of their voices coming from her room.

"Is anyone else besides us looking for Kallisto?" Deo was persistent.

"Yes, I just deployed a team."

I was not only shocked but frustrated that Calix and Carrigan had been working for Kallisto. Thank goodness for Taurik and his friends. If they hadn't been there for me, I wouldn't have had any true friends in my time of need.

Taurik. I wondered what Kallisto had done with him. Probably locked him away. I wasn't worried that she was going to harm him because she needed him to get to me.

I must have looked forlorn because Aunt Maggie took my hand saying, "It's okay, sweetie. I'm sure they'll find your boyfriend."

"Boyfriend!" Zander sneered.

Oh, no. I gazed at him, and the intense anger in his eyes segued into intense longing. I was glad Deo chose that moment to take charge.

"Meda, you can tell me later where you and the others have been hiding. But right now, we need to get a little food into Omega." Professor Omega looked like he could have lost his footing in a gust of wind.

"Or a lot of food into him," Rhaine added.

Deo centered on me. "And we have a celebration to plan for our long-lost daughter!" He took my face in his hands. The promise of a new future filled his eyes. "Aspasia will never be the same."

"Aspasia ceased being the same the instant I arrived." My own candor surprised me.

"Touché, Princess. Shall I show you to your palace now?"

I smiled. "That would be lovely." I took his hand as he guided me toward my new life as Princess of Aspasia.

End of Book 2

GLOSSARY

Abervania – an educational institution located in the prip of Vashia.

Alternator – One who shares an existence with another person, but neither can inhabit reality at the same time.

Amourite – the brain-stimulating element that gives Aspasians perfect recall.

Anthilomy – or *heart anthilomy*, an involuntary visual representation of loved ones.

Aphotics – beings who control aphotic power.

Aphotic energy – type of energy that is drawn from unknown sources in the universe.

Aphotology – study of aphotic energy.

Appenda-port – type of transportation device composed of conversion stones its holder awakens.

Aspasia – galaxy ruled by Deo Clevist.

Aspasian Investigatory Force (AIF) – equivalent of the USA's FBI.

Aspasian Technology – technology used solely by Aspasians.

Aspasiars – Aspasian soldier.

Bilbop – light-weight technological device which stores up to two hundred pounds of its owner's possessions.

Bottomless Pits – specialty drink that increases aphotic entranx; bitter in taste.

Bowdian soup – type of soup with vegetables and three types of meat.

Canceller – a being who counteracts the effects of any power.

Chastology – study of chaste energy.

Clevists – Deo and Rhaine, King and Queen of Aspasia; also includes Deo's brother Prodrian, who was killed after attempting to overthrow the Aspasian government.

Confidi entranx – type of entranx energy that permits its user to control the levels of confidence in those around him or her.

Consummation – equivalent to lunch.

Conversion stones – stones which are awakened by entranx energy that correlates with its inner power type; used to help students discover their power types and subsequently used as the inner power source for students' appenda-ports.

Creechuh – equivalent to a creature.

Crozii – blank space to be shaped according to the dreams of a private owner; can range from a few acres to an entire world; an Aspasian citizen must be granted permission by the government before taking ownership of a crozii, which can serve as an entire world apart from Aspasia.

Dark phoenix – almighty phoenix spirit composed of 2,000 individual phoenix spirits forced into it through the aphotic process of plyxing.

Delutz – crozii located on the outer reaches of Aspasia.

Doppelganger – an apparition or double of a living person.

Encourager – being who can empathize with any person.

Entrax energy – type of energy that inhabits all Aspasians and grants them power.

Entrax pattern – distinct biological pattern, like genetic makeup, composed of an Aspasian's entranx energy; determines power types.

Femino essence – concentrated essence that enhances one's feminine qualities.

Fiaszo – type of food composed of fias, a nutritious plant in Aspasia; when prepared for consumption, looks similar to a glob of Laffy-taffy.

Grobe – Aspasian name for a massive athletic complex.

History of Aspasia – study of Aspasian history dating all the way back to the discovery of Aspasia by the original founders.

In-betweener – type of Aspasian who serves as an intermediary for other Aspasians' powers.

Innate Capability – ability to understand any concept without having to invest time in learning it.

Jeex – type of creechuh that looks similar to a porcupine and burrows in the ground for most of its life; also a popular Aspasian delicacy with a sweet taste.

Liphon – Aspasian spy who goes AWOL and uses his or her government connections to gain an upper hand.

Logic – study of how the mind thinks.

Lyvites – Aspasian delicacy comprised of crab in a lime juice with quinoa.

Metaprites – cheerleaders.

Morbids – being who sacrifices his or her health to wield power from an unknown source in the universe; for them, telling a secret leads to death.

Orgratium – secretary.

Paltakeet – bird from the northern quasian of Planesia; its eggs are used in the delicacy Planesian Pevdots.

Pampolonian Steak – Aspasian delicacy comprised of steak prepared in butter with a cream sauce over steamed carrots and potatoes.

Phoenix – a spirit composed of emotions it takes on as a result of its holder's emotions.
Phoenix-holders – beings whose entranx patterns are conducive to holding a phoenix spirit within their bodies.

Pinkest Pucker – specialty drink largely comprised of strawberries and copious amount of femino essence; recommended for chastes.

Planesian Pevdots – Aspasian dish made up of Paltakeet eggs.

Plyxing – process in which aphotic energy is used to strip a phoenix spirit from a person's body and insert it into another body.

Power Practice – type of class in which fight formations are studied in relation to individual students' power types.

Quintessence – type of class in which the relationship between entranx energy and essence are studied.

Quizeen – the equivalent of a princess, but she is ruler over an entire quasian; the only ones above her in power are the gods.

Quasian – the equivalent of a country.

Sitzoscope – magical flashlight only attuned to chaste students and whose power source is chaste energy.

Vashia – prip where Abervania is located.

Whisper-chasing – type of ability in which its wielder can whisper words into his or her hand before releasing them to the words' intended listener without any chance of being overheard.

ASPASIAN EMPIRE GOVERNMENT STRUCTURE (In order of decreasing jurisdiction)

POSITION	JURISDICTION
Gods	Entirety of Aspasia
Quiziar/Quizeen	Quasian
Vito/Vita	Vitars
Zylar/Zyleen	Zylos
Zotiats/Zoteens	Zots
Propiars/Propeens	Prips

About the Author

Clay F. Turner is an Arkansas State University graduate with a Bachelor of Arts in political science and a minor in Spanish. He is originally from Leachville, Arkansas and started writing the *Lodesyia* series in 8th grade. His first book, *Lodesyia*, was published in 2014.

Through his writing, Clay hopes that kids perceive that the power exhibited by his characters is just as real in their own lives. After all, every child has untapped potential to become whoever they want.